The Tutor

Bonnie Dee

Copyright © 2019 Bonnie Dee
All rights reserved.
ISBN-13: 978-1-7991-1375-1

CONTENTS

1	Chapter 1	1
2	Chapter 2	16
3	Chapter 3	25
4	Chapter 4	32
5	Chapter 5	37
6	Chapter 6	44
7	Chapter 7	52
8	Chapter 8	62
9	Chapter 9	69
10	Chapter 10	81
11	Chapter 11	90
12	Chapter 12	98
13	Chapter 13	109
14	Chapter 14	123
15	Chapter 15e	135
16	Chapter 16	140
17	Chapter 17	149
18	Chapter 18	161
19	Chapter 19	170
20	Chapter 20	181
21	Chapter 21	186
22	Chapter 22	194
23	Chapter 23	209

CHAPTER 1

Yorkshire, England 1893

When I first saw Allinson Hall looming dark and foreboding in the distance, I feared I approached a lunatic asylum rather than a family home. The sprawling gray building appeared hewn from the great rocks that littered the moors and as ominous as the threatening clouds overhead. *What a lovely place to raise children.* Little did I know that an even bleaker darkness than the house possessed resided in the manor's owner, Sir Richard Allinson.

My heart kept time with the horses' hooves, moving faster now that the animals approached their warm stable and hay. The carriage wheels banged over a rut in the road, making my teeth click together painfully. I pressed my cheek against the cold glass of the carriage window and squinted into the gathering gloom, trying to get a better view of my future home. As the carriage rolled down an incline, the manor house disappeared in a fold of land. These moors might appear level but were actually rolling, not quite the open vista I had imagined.

I sat back on the barely padded seat that offered no protection to my travel-weary bones and reviewed the history I'd embroidered for myself. What would my new employer think if he knew how little experience I'd had as a tutor—which is to say, none? Based on falsified references, I was about to take up a post on a North Country estate imparting knowledge to twin boys. How difficult could it be to teach two nine-year-olds the basic subjects? Meanwhile, I'd be living in the lap of luxury through winter, which could be cold and harsh in the grimy London neighborhood where I'd previously resided.

My communication with Richard Allinson had taken place through letters and his solicitor. I had yet to meet this widowed father in person. My tension at the rather large lie I was about to perpetrate grew with each passing mile. I became convinced he'd take one look at me and see through my paper-thin story. The Graham Cowrie I'd created via testimonials and letters of recommendation reflected little of the real me, but I would embrace this role and climb a new rung of the ladder out of the slum where I'd been born.

The carriage bounced over another jarring rut. My back twinged from far too many hours of riding in train cars and then this rickety carriage from some bygone era. Every time I looked out the window, there was nothing to see but grassy moors and folds of billowing gray clouds. What family would choose to settle in such a place? But apparently, the Allinsons had occupied the manor for generations, a lineage stretching back to the Tudors, I believed. The family owned land worked by tenants, factories in other parts of England, and Lord knew what else to keep the great beast of an estate fed.

Now several lighted windows winked in the gathering darkness. I couldn't make out the details of the sprawling house, which again jutted from the land, but its hulking shape against the twilight sky fostered an air of foreboding. Distant thunder rumbled and lightning flashed like a portent of danger. A cold shiver raced through me. Though I pretended to scoff at tales shared by my several spiritualist friends, in truth I believed in ghosts and spirits. And if ever a building appeared haunted, it was this one.

I wrapped my arms tight around my body and pulled my chin deeper into the turned-up collar of my coat. The fabric was too thin for winter, but I couldn't afford to buy another. The house loomed closer until it filled my vision, blotting out the horizon. My heart raced as if I were running alongside the horses.

Only a few lighted windows signaled anyone lived in this monstrosity. It was composed of the stone walls and turrets of the original medieval fortress with more recently cobbled-on wings, *recent* being a relative term that probably encompassed the last few hundred years.

High in the largest tower—which no doubt would've been the guard tower in a bygone era when attacking armies threatened—a single bright beam of light drew my attention. But when I looked up the cylindrical column, there was no light after all. Perhaps window glass had reflected a lightning flash.

The carriage passed through a gap in a stone wall. I had no more opportunity to ponder strange lights or eerie fantasies of the spirits that might dwell in a building so steeped in layers of time. I must focus on presenting myself to Sir Richard Allinson and bringing complete confidence to my exaggerated history. He would believe my lies only if I believed them myself.

The horses' hooves clattered on stone as the carriage reached the grand courtyard, and the coachman brought them to a halt. I reached for the door handle. Before I could grasp it, the coachman, who'd introduced himself as Drover, opened the door. He spoke not a word, merely stood like a sentinel, waiting. What a jolly welcome to my new home.

I sucked in a lungful of the bracing air before climbing out of the shelter like a moth emerging from its cocoon. Once I left the carriage behind, I must embrace my new life and identity completely. A terrifying thought.

The moment my shoes hit the flagstones, icy wind swirled my coat around my legs, binding them so I could scarcely walk. It blew my hat from my head, and scoured my face with grit and sleet. Drover hurried to retrieve my hat, his black coat flapping around him like a sail.

I gazed at the wide, ornately carved door under the imposing portico resting on stone pillars. This would be the largest, grandest building I'd ever been in, barring museums and a tour of the Tower of London. I must behave as if I were used to working in a house like this, as if the surroundings didn't impress me and my knees weren't knocking together. *Play the part. Become the tutor.*

The coachman returned to hand me my hat just as one side of the double door creaked open on mighty hinges with the slow majesty of a drawbridge admitting entrance to a castle. Light spilled from inside to illuminate the wet flagstones.

"Best hurry in," Drover said at last.

"Yes." I forced my weak legs to march across the courtyard toward the doorway, where a black-suited figure waited. A butler, of course. My coworker, so to speak. I knew little of the hierarchy of the staff in a country estate, but had reviewed some of the protocol with my friend Annie, who used to be in service. With luck, I wouldn't make any huge gaffes to reveal I'd had no experience.

"Good evening, Mr. Cowrie."

My bold steps faltered at the butler's funereal tone and gaunt, jaundiced face, hardly more than skin stretched over bone. He appeared more of a talking skeleton than a living man.

"Good evening." I managed not to cringe away from his frightening figure as I passed. And then I lost all power of speech as I gazed around the museum of a hallway. Worn and faded tapestries covered the walls. Two full suits of armor faced one another like ghostly sentries. One had to walk past their raised double-bladed axes in order to proceed. This place was in every aspect the gothic monstrosity of the pulp novels I'd read. In those novels, the ingénue inevitably regretted her decision to take a governess position at an isolated estate on a windswept moor. I gave a little grimace of a smile at the thought.

If I'd stayed in my job at the print shop, I'd be enjoying the end of a work day in the pub next door about now. But my typesetting position had offered little possibility of advancement, which was why I'd responded to an advertisement requiring the services of a tutor. I'd been seduced by the prestige such a job would add to my résumé *and* by the higher pay and a chance to winter in rich accommodations. Hah! The hall was drafty and cold. The stone walls and flagstone floor beneath a thin carpet radiated the chill of a tomb. It was highly doubtful the rest of the old pile would be any more welcoming, and I'd be lucky if I was given a lump of coal to heat my bedchamber.

I turned to ask the butler his name and found the man had evaporated. No. Not evaporated, but shifted position with feline swiftness, for when I faced forward again, he was right in front of me. I jumped and nearly squeaked in surprise before I asked, "Shall I get my bags, Mister…?"

"Smithers." His bloodless lips barely moved, and his face remained masklike. "The boy will bring in your luggage."

Gaslights illuminated the hall. At least that much technology had made it into this mausoleum. But Smithers carried a paraffin lantern as he led me down a narrower and very dim hallway. We passed darkened rooms, which would no doubt be a parlor, a sitting room, a dining room, and all the other extra rooms wealthy people required in order to live to their satisfaction.

I felt like I should ask him questions about the household, but

Smithers's silence was so intimidating, it stalled the words in my throat. I plodded after him, a refugee taken in from a storm and begrudgingly offered a room for the night. In a novel, that traveler might not live until morning, or he'd have to battle the evil force in the eerie mansion.

My wild imagination made me shiver as I followed Smithers up several flights of stairs and down another hallway. The butler stopped in front of a door, and I nearly ran into him.

"This will be your chamber. Master Whitney and Master Clive share the bedroom just over there. The schoolroom is at the end of the hall. You shall meet the young masters and the staff tomorrow. Sir Richard is currently abroad but should return within a week."

I nearly sighed aloud. At least I would have time to adjust to my surroundings before meeting the master of the house. Yet at the same time, I wished to have the formal interview over with. It wasn't too late for the man to send me packing, and I'd be lingering in limbo until I passed muster.

Smithers opened the door, and I entered a small bedchamber dominated by a tall, old-fashioned bed draped in curtains. Dickens's Ebenezer Scrooge could've rested in that bed while awaiting the ghosts of Christmas past, present, and future. Coal smoke stung my nose. The fire on the grate puffed wisps of smoke into the room as if the flue was partially blocked. But at least the bedroom was vaguely warmer than the hallway and definitely warmer than my London flat would have been on a night like this.

I looked at Smithers, who stood solemnly beside me, perhaps waiting for my response, or else he'd died standing with his rheumy eyes wide open.

"Thank you. This is a lovely room." It wasn't, but I had to say something. What I really wanted to ask about was dinner, and the mere thought of food made my stomach growl.

"You may go to the kitchen, where Cook has set by a plate for you."

"Ah. That would be greatly appreciated. I was afraid I might have to wait for breakfast." I chuckled, and the smoky air swallowed the mirthful sound. I stopped laughing.

Footsteps echoed in the hallway, and I eagerly looked toward the sign of another living soul inhabiting the house. A young man entered bearing my valise and trunk. His forehead sloped straight into his skull, leaving little room for a brain, and the vacant look in his eyes suggested he was feeble-minded. The youth set down my luggage while sneaking furtive glances at me.

"Thank you. I'm Graham Cowrie. How do you do?" I greeted him, sticking out my hand to shake.

The footman stepped back as if I might slap him. I dropped my hand.

"Don't mind Tom. He's slow-witted but harmless. He will grow used to your presence." Smithers dismissed the youth with a jerk of his head, and Tom scurried out.

After that, Smithers showed me the way to the water closet—thank God for that amenity. I'd feared I was in the land of chamber pots and no proper plumbing. Then he led the twisting, turning way down to the kitchen. I sat at one end of the large servants' hall table and studied my surroundings as I ate the cold plate of meat, cheese, and bread. I tried to imagine the place crowded with maids, footmen, a cook, and a housekeeper, but couldn't manage it. The room was silent and empty, and I felt the entire house was peopled only by ghosts. It didn't help that mysterious sounds came from all around: creaking wood, wheezing pipes, wind rattling window frames, icy rain pelting the panes. I was in the belly of an enormous beast settling down for the night—and preparing to digest me.

Smithers informed me of the schedule of meals in the house. "Yours will be taken with the boys in the nursery."

I'd expected that. Other than lessons, I'd have little to do with the boys and would have many hours to relax. Perhaps I'd chip away at writing that novel that had never gotten beyond the fantasizing stage. I frowned. "But I'm their tutor, not their nursemaid."

Smithers's lips moved without awakening his dead eyes at all. "You might find procedures at Allinson Hall a bit unorthodox. The boys' nanny left some time past, and since then, they've been rather left to their own devices. It will be your duty to give the boys a more structured regimen. Your room is near theirs so you may be more aware of their comings and goings."

Smithers's curled lip displayed a whiff of emotion. He disapproved of the boys running wild and wanted someone to control the little blighters. I wasn't merely going to be teaching a few classes but acting as jailer to a pair of motherless, nannyless ruffians. The pieces shifted into place as I saw the picture of why I'd been so easily accepted for this position with little interviewing or examination of my history.

I swallowed a bite of meat that stuck in my throat. "I understand."

Smithers rocked back on his heels. "I recommend you retire directly after your repast. The young masters wake early and will be eager to meet you, I'm sure. You may begin their lessons tomorrow morning."

The butler left me to finish my meal alone and find my way through the labyrinth of a house back to my room. Good God, what had I fallen into? I'd pictured myself explaining equations and world history to two bright-eyed cherubs eager to soak up the knowledge I imparted. Now it sounded as if I might be in charge of the spawn of Satan if Smithers's lip curling was any indication.

I finished every crumb of my meal, put the plate in a sink and pumped a glass of water from the tap. Gaslights, indoor plumbing, *and* running water—this place had all the modern amenities, I chided myself. A bloke could do much worse, and I had in the past.

How bad could the little urchins be anyway? I'd run with a vicious mob of street rats as a lad. Clive and Whitney Allinson would seem princely little nobs in comparison.

I returned the way Smithers and I had come. I thought I'd paid attention when he led me to the kitchen, but I must have taken a wrong turn in one of the passageways, for I could not find my way to my room. I padded down one darkened hallway after another, passing closed doors I feared to open.

I grew ever more lost and stopped worrying about walking in on someone, since all the rooms seemed empty. I peeked into one and found a study dominated by a dark mahogany desk. I held up the lantern Smithers had given me to study several shelves of books—titles concerning agriculture and land management that looked dull as dirt. Then I noticed a portrait hanging above the fireplace.

A fair-haired woman with a rather round face stared back at me: Lavinia Allinson as a new bride just beginning her abbreviated life, the poor thing. Though she'd smiled for the artist, a vague sadness haunted her blue eyes, and I wondered about this woman who seemed unhappy despite all she possessed.

I'll do my best to teach your tykes, I promised her before backing out of the room.

Beginning to enjoy my late-night exploration, I moved up a floor and peered into several bedrooms and sitting rooms with cloth-draped furniture. Moving deeper into the original fortress portion of the house, I came across a medieval chapel. I imagined lords and ladies praying here, living their lives for generations before the Allinsons took possession. The weight of time and history felt profound in the quiet night in a tiny chapel with several wooden pews and a granite altar. If I were a religious man, someplace like this might move me to speak with God.

I left the room and continued my tour, climbing another flight and heading in the direction I believed the inhabited chambers lay. The next corridor seemed familiar. I walked more confidently, until a sound stopped me. I held my breath and listened. A soft sobbing wafted through the air. *Wind in the eaves*, I thought, but damned if it didn't sound like a woman crying.

A frigid draft blew down the hall, and I hurried on. The scent of coal smoke and light from under a door signaled I'd nearly reached my destination. But footsteps seemed to echo my own, pattering after me. I halted again and looked over my shoulder. Nothing but shadows in the hall behind me. This time, eerie whispering drifted down the passage. Quiet little voices. Children, perhaps?

My momentary jolt of panic subsided. It seemed my new charges were following me, perhaps simply trying to get a look at their tutor, but probably trying to give me a scare. Little scamps. I couldn't let them know they'd affected me, or they'd be out of control with their tricks. I continued nonchalantly to my room and went inside.

"Good night, boys," I called softly down the hall before I shut my door.

My trunk and a couple of valises sat on the floor of the room. Far too wide awake to think of settling down in that tall, lumpy bed, I unpacked everything and put my clothes in the wardrobe and bureau. Some were my own cheap suits. Others I'd purchased as a wardrobe I deemed more appropriate for Graham Cowrie, a young gentleman whose family had been financially ruined.

My own background was considerably less sophisticated. I'd emerged from the cocoon of Joe Green by meeting someone who gave me a helping hand, studying hard and changing my accent. I'd been Graham Cowrie for a while now, but I'd given this new incarnation of Graham a more prestigious lineage. Would've been wiser to keep the story slightly closer to the truth, but I couldn't resist the faded gentility of the man I'd created.

I set my brush, comb, and shaving kit on top of the bureau, stuffed the valises inside the empty trunk, which neatly fit under the bed, and added another lump of coal to the fire. Then there was nothing left to do but change into my nightshirt and climb into bed.

I'd barely pushed my bare feet and legs between chilly sheets when something scratched my bare skin. Prickling sharp things tore at my flesh. I threw back the covers to find the forest floor arrayed on my bed—a smattering of pine needles, twigs, and a rather large bramble with nasty hooked thorns, one of which had snagged my shin. I carefully unhooked it, leaving a blood-oozing welt behind. I got up, swept nature's bounty off the mattress, and disposed of it in the fire.

Watching the dried needles and briars burn, I cursed the jackanapes who'd played the prank. I could hardly wait until morning to meet them. This was exactly the sort of prank I'd gotten up to as a lad. If the twins thought they could best me, that I was a lily-livered, weak sort, I'd take 'em down a peg.

Whitney and Clive Allinson's worst nightmare was coming for them.

CHAPTER 2

When I finally pried open my reluctant eyes, the light streaming in my window told me I'd greatly overslept. Smithers had warned me I was expected to take breakfast with the boys and see they washed and dressed themselves neatly. My easy winter of playing a tutor was apparently not going to be easy at all.

A knock at the door interrupted my lounging and worrying, and I leaped out of bed and pulled on my robe before answering.

A woman stood on my doorstep. No. Not a woman. An Amazon. She towered over me. The abundant hair swept into a pile on her head only made her appear taller and as if she were wearing some sort of massive turban. She gazed down at me disapprovingly, telling me silently how much she despised slugabeds.

"Mr. Cowrie. I am Mrs. Growler, the housekeeper."

I bowed slightly, then offered my hand to shake. I wasn't sure what a man in my position was meant to do. Was she my superior or more of a peer since a tutor's duties didn't directly fall under the housekeeper's jurisdiction?

Mrs. Growler, an apt name, ignored my hand and glared into my eyes. "The boys are already up and outdoors, playing in the gardens. It's my understanding you've come here to take their behavior in hand. I suggest you get to it—if you can catch them."

"Yes, ma'am. I apologize for rising so late. It won't happen again. I had a taxing journey." I offered my widest, most appealing smile. It usually worked to soothe ladies' ruffled feathers, and many a man's as well if they were inclined to be swayed by boyish charm.

But Mrs. Growler wasn't moved. "I hope you're up to the task." She sniffed and stalked away.

After pouring chilly water from the pitcher into the basin, I shaved and washed as clean as one could in a basin. The brown tweed suit I'd planned for my first day suggested sober studiousness. I'd considered adding gold-rimmed spectacles to complete the picture, but that had seemed a stretch. Pretending to need glasses only added unnecessary complexity to my role.

I regarded myself in the shaving mirror. Serious blue-gray eyes stared back at me. Before leaving London, I'd had my brown hair cut well above collar length. I wore a sharp side part and slicked the bangs to sweep just above my forehead, a much more clean-cut, spartan style than I would normally wear. Men loved a curly headed lad, and I enjoyed feeling a strong hand comb through my locks.

I'd also begun to cultivate a thin moustache, but it was coming in so light and sparse, I thought I might give up and shave it off.

I nodded at my reflection. "Definitely a schoolteacher's demeanor. Now to find and capture my students."

What does every boy know and every man forget? That having fun is the prime purpose of life. I recalled Mr. Twain's Tom Sawyer, who convinced all the boys in town to play a game of whitewashing a fence and pay him for the privilege. I would entice my quarry by inventing a game they couldn't resist. The best way to get Whitney and Clive to come to me was to suggest I'd unlocked some secret to fun, and, if they were lucky, I might teach it to them.

In that case, the sober teacher attire was not the costume I needed. Instead I put on a thick knit jumper and corduroy trousers, donned my warmest pair of socks and the Wellington boots I'd wisely purchased before heading into the northern wilds. I would go outdoors, where my prospective students might spy on me from a distance while I played the most exciting, energetic, amusing game imaginable. The rules I invented didn't have to make sense, so long as the boys believed I was having much more fun doing my activity than they were having at theirs. I'd woo them close, then clobber them with learning.

Downstairs I found Smithers, who retrieved my coat. If he had any opinion on the casual attire I was wearing, he didn't express it as he pointed me toward a back door leading to the gardens.

I stepped out into a breeze balmier than the previous evening's sleety wind, though still cold by any stretch of the imagination. I walked along leaf-drifted paths, past dried-up fountains and an occasional moss-covered bench or statue. The summer's plantings had gone to seed and rattled like dry bones at my passing. The wind mourned through naked branches, and I fastened the top button on my too-thin coat.

Beyond the gardens was wilder land. Not yet the moor but a wide-open patch where one might play cricket or some other athletic game, if the grass were properly mowed. I began to pace out this overgrown field, all the while sneaking looks around for my two young charges. I caught a glimpse of a blue jacket, which quickly disappeared behind a toolshed. A fair head bobbed up above a low hedge and disappeared again like an agitated gopher.

I dropped the ball I'd brought with me onto the ground and began to waffle it back and forth between my feet. What subject might interest two nine-year-olds? Most boys, like their adult counterparts, loved playing with armies of soldiers and fleets of ships. As I kicked the ball high in the air, then caught it, I called out the names of famous battles and the dates they'd occurred. I clapped my hands and caught the ball before running to the next base I'd trampled into the grass. This time I shouted the names, in order, of as many kings of England as I could remember and again tossed the ball high and bellowed a war cry before catching it. I howled as I charged toward the next base. Behaving like a madman, I indulged in the sort of loud, insane game only young children would invent or understand.

Another peek showed me two pale, very round faces poking out from either side of a wide tree trunk. Whitney and Clive had moved closer. As I played by myself, they crept from the tree to a nearby bush, where they dropped to all fours like small animals.

I threw the ball high in the air and recited the names of the ruling Caesars, as many as I could before the ball touched ground again. It bounced. I caught it and quoted a poem while dribbling the ball between my feet all the way to the first base.

"Over the mountains of the moon, down in the valley of the shadow. Ride, boldly ride, the shade replied, if you seek for Eldorado."

I was out of breath. Would my ranting and ball throwing be sufficient to bring the boys out of hiding? I glanced over to find two small figures in overly large coats, one green, one blue, standing on the sidelines of my imaginary field, staring at me.

I threw the ball toward them. Without hesitation, the slightly taller and even more moon-faced of the two caught it between red-mittened hands.

"Quick, what did the cow jump over?" I demanded.

"The moon," the boy replied, too shocked not to reply.

"Good. Now bounce the ball, spin around, and catch it, then ask your own question." I clapped my hands. "Quick, quick. Hurry. No time to waste."

The taller brother bounced the ball hard, whirled in a circle, then ran to catch the ball.

"Shout your question," I reminded him.

"Um, what's the capital of Portugal?" He threw the ball back at me.

I caught it and answered, "Lisbon," then bounced it with my head toward the other twin. "What's the name of England's queen?" I kept it easy.

The boy didn't put up his hands, and the ball bounced off his chest. His twin caught the ricochet and answered the question. "Queen Victoria. Clive doesn't talk," he explained.

"Oh." That was news no one had bothered to share with me. "But can he catch a ball?"

Whitney, the talking one, threw the ball to Clive. This time the boy caught it, stared at it, and gave it a tremendous kick that sent the ball careening into a very tall and thick hedge.

"Strong kick." I trotted over to retrieve the ball from under the yew, scratching my hands before I located it. I half expected when I turned around the twins would've evaporated like smoke, but they still stood there, staring at me.

A little charge of smug satisfaction ignited in me. I'd caught their attention and held their interest. Maybe I would do all right as a teacher.

"What fleet did Sir Francis Drake demolish?" I called out as I threw the ball to Whitney again.

"The Spanish Armada." He shot a look at Clive. Some silent communication passed between them, and Clive nodded.

"Defeated in 1588," Whit added as if speaking for his brother.

Eerie little buggers.

Whit threw the ball to his twin, who kicked it high in the air, forcing me to run to catch it.

Whit posed his next question. "Have you ever been to Buckingham Palace?"

It wasn't schoolroom related, but I answered anyway. "I've been past the fence. They don't let common folk inside to tour it."

"What about the Tower?"

I ignored the fact he was breaking my rules by asking more than one question. If the boys were interested in me, that was a positive sign.

"I took a tour once. It's a very dismal place."

"They used to torture people. The two boy princes, Edward and Richard, were prisoners there." Whit drew closer, still gazing at me with the nearly transparent blue eyes both boys possessed. "They still haunt the Tower, along with many others."

"Ghastly and exciting tales to be sure." I bounced the ball on my knee a couple of times and threw it at Clive, who flanked me on the left. Now *I* felt like an animal being stalked by two rather malevolent little jackals.

"What's your favorite color?" I demanded of Clive, piercing him with a stare I hoped would startle an answer out of him. "Is it blue?" I asked, since he was the one who wore a blue coat.

Pale eyes under straight brows and a fringe of wheat-blond hair glared at me. He threw the ball back—hard—straight at my chest. It stung my hands when I intercepted it.

All right, then. No more questions. I'd let Clive reveal himself in his own time. He was going to be the trickier one.

For the next ten minutes or so, I engaged the boys in my silly game. They raced around chasing the ball with intense fervor. Whit spoke for both of them, asking and answering questions that ranged from history to astronomy to folklore. In very short order, I learned he was smart and surprisingly well-read for a young boy who'd not yet had formal schooling. I wondered who had taught him to read.

Just as I was patting myself on the back for how I'd been able to coax them out of their shyness, both boys suddenly froze. Red-faced and puffing, they stared beyond me. I turned to see what had drawn their attention, and my own body went rigid.

A figure straight out of a gothic novel approached us, striding like a nightmare vision. Tall, broad-shouldered, wearing a black greatcoat and knee-high boots, the man could have easily played the role of a dastardly villain in an operetta. As he drew nearer and I studied the hard planes of his handsome face, I changed my mind. He was definitely the brooding hero of the story, a man mired in personal misery and darkness and just waiting for the heroine to lead him to the light with her love. *Sigh.*

That was my flight of fancy as I regarded my new employer. My heart pitter-pattered, and other parts of my anatomy went hard as I smiled in greeting. "Good day. Sir Richard, I presume?"

Then the man spoke, and I landed on earth with a sharp thud.

"What is going on here? I don't believe I hired you to run amok with my children. They should be in the schoolroom this time of day, learning their times tables and Latin."

Black slashes of eyebrows drew together over deep brown eyes that glittered as they caught the sunlight. Gorgeous and gloomy, dark and dangerous looking—just the sort of man who featured in my fantasies. A wave of powerful attraction surged through me, and I could hardly collect my wits to form a sentence.

"This being my first day, sir, I thought it would be worthwhile to create a rapport with the boys while learning a little about their level of knowledge. The modern approach is for students to learn organically rather than recite by rote," I lied. Let him think this was some progressive technique all the best people were using rather than simply me flying by the seat of my pants.

Not wanting Whit and Clive to overhear and think I'd manipulated them, I lowered my voice a little. "Once trust is built, I've found my pupils are much more willing and eager to learn."

I needn't have worried about revealing my intentions to the twins. When I glanced over my shoulder, they'd both evaporated like steam.

The master of the house raked a hot glare over me from head to toe, leaving my flesh scored and burning.

His lips compressed. "Modern approach. It appears more as if you've fallen in with the savages. From now on, I expect to find my sons learning their lessons in the schoolroom. They've had free rein for far too long."

Another scathing glance flicked over me like a lash. "Take the boys in hand, set yourself to rights, and come to my study, where we will review my expectations for your employment."

Sir Richard turned to walk away, and I—governed by too little sense and too well developed a sense of humor—called after him, "You might consider joining the savages for a while yourself, sir. They're an entertaining lot."

He stopped walking, and I caught my breath. I'd gone and done it, got myself sacked on the very first day. I'd be on a train back to London before the hour was up.

Sir Richard slowly turned to stare at me with those sizzling eyes. I could've crumpled like a cheap suit under the onslaught of his gaze, but forced myself to straighten my spine and smile back at him.

The man blinked. He didn't say another word, simply faced forward and continued on toward the house.

I exhaled loudly and shook my head at my own foolishness. Bowing and scraping simply weren't my strong suit, and this wouldn't be the first position I'd lost by letting my tongue wag at its will.

I searched the area for the twins. We'd been playing ball in an open field. They couldn't have returned to the gardens without passing their father, and there weren't that many hiding places. A quick scan revealed a splash of blue squatting behind a stump and a green coat belly down to the earth.

I frowned. Did their father discipline the boys with beatings? I couldn't imagine why else they'd have gone to ground at his appearance rather than, at the very least, greeting him politely. It was odd Sir Richard hadn't seemed surprised by their rude behavior or called them to come to him. What sort of strange family was this?

Not my place to worry about it, I realized. For likely I'd be gone soon.

"Whitney. Clive," I called. "Come here, please." I spoke as if I expected to be obeyed, and damned if it didn't work. Whitney rose from the grass, and Clive emerged from behind the stump. They trudged slowly toward me through the long grass.

"Seems we'll need to resume our game indoors, lads. Will you come to the schoolroom with me?" I tossed the ball from hand to hand.

The brothers exchanged another long silent communication, then looked at me.

Whitney nodded. "All right."

I felt as if I'd won a small victory as my new charges meekly fell in step with me. I shot the ball to Clive, who tossed it to Whit, who threw it back to me, and we continued to play together as we marched toward whatever punishment Sir Richard had in store.

CHAPTER 3

I escorted the boys to what had probably been their nursery before conversion to schoolroom and play area, and bid them good-bye. I might not see them again, but I'd do my best to placate Sir Richard and keep my post.

"Time for me to tidy up a bit and meet with your father," I said. "While I'm gone, will you do something for me?"

Clive started sidling out the door at the mention of a task. Whit frowned and scuffed his shoe back and forth on the floor. "What sort of thing?"

I sat on one of the small chairs so I was on eye level with the boys. "Here's the thing. I have dreams of becoming a writer. I've been penning a novel, and I'd value your feedback on it," I extemporized, not possessing any such thing, since my tales had gone no further than my brain. "I'd feel more comfortable showing you my work if I could read something of yours in return. Would you both be willing to write a very short story to share with me? A paragraph would do. Whatever you'd like, but preferably something frightening. Those are my favorite types of stories."

Whit's eyes lit up. "Could it be about a grave robber and a resurrected corpse? And the corpse goes after the man and tears him to bits?"

I exaggerated a shiver. "That would be very ghoulish indeed."

I looked past him at Clive, whose interest was piqued enough to at least make him pause in the doorway. "Or perhaps a funny story. Maybe about some children who have a new governess they don't like so they play tricks on her to try to drive her off. Maybe she turns the tables on them because she's actually a witch."

Clive gazed at me with an expression that was the spitting image of his father's—disdain mingled with disbelief that anyone could be so stupid. Sour-faced Clive made his brother appear positively jovial in comparison, although neither boy had as yet cracked a true smile.

I left them to do whatever they were going to do, sit and write or run outdoors to play some more, and made my way downstairs. I had to ask a maid to point me toward Sir Richard's study. The girl barely spoke above a whisper as she explained which passages to take, and she looked at me with pitying eyes as if I were going to face Lucifer himself.

I thanked her as she returned to her dusting and tried to follow directions down one gloomy corridor after another. The house was a crazy maze laid out illogically, easy to get lost in. I spotted a few of the rooms I'd explored the previous night and realized I'd gotten turned around and wandered into the old fortress. There was that chapel again and farther down the hall, a door left partially open.

Curiosity made me peek inside. A spiral staircase led away into darkness. This must be the massive corner tower, the one in which I thought I saw a light upon my arrival. I'd probably never have an opportunity to explore the intriguing place again after Sir Richard was through with me, so I walked up a few steps. The stone was worn to smoothness and slightly dipped in the center from generations of people winding their way up and down. I imagined guards taking their shift at the top of the tower. Sharp-eyed watchmen ready to sound a warning of approaching danger.

Again I sensed the weight of time and years, heavy and almost palpable, somber and serious. I stopped three steps up, unable to take another, and that weight became something else, a nearly indescribable feeling of sorrow and negativity that seemed to flow into me from somewhere outside myself. I wanted to weep. Cold seeped into my flesh and bones, and a scent—slightly sweet like flowers but with a note of decay—filled my nose.

A whisper of sound floated through the still air to land on my ears. It was like the sobbing I thought I'd heard last night, but even softer, more of a feeling than an audible noise. Then it was gone.

I listened but heard nothing more in the chilly tower. Shaking off my sluggish inertia and sensation of anxiety, I retreated down the steps. Time to face something truly frightening—the master of the house.

Leaving the door ajar as I'd found it, I walked down the hall. I'd gone only a few yards when a thud resounded in the corridor behind me. I spun around. The door I'd left open had shut all on its own.

Heart pounding, I trotted faster toward the inhabited portion of the sprawling old pile. The masonry grew fresher, the fusty smell of mold and age diminished, and soon I stood in front of the door to Sir Richard's study, the room I'd looked into the previous night.

With the trepidation of a schoolboy facing the headmaster, I rapped at the door.

"Come in."

A simple enough command that set off an oversized reaction in me. Predominantly fear that I would lose my post, or worse, that Allinson had learned my credentials were a lie and would turn me over to the authorities, but also an undercurrent of excitement and a ridiculous frisson of lust at the timbre of the man's voice. He spoke with the cultured accent of aristocracy, yet there was a sort of roughness in his deep voice that somehow suggested to me a man who worked with his hands and wasn't afraid to get them dirty. The best of both worlds, educated intellect coupled with a workingman's raw strength and vitality.

"Idiot!" My insane musings had no basis in fact. I tended to indulge myself in little fantasies that real life mostly didn't measure up to.

I opened the door and entered.

The master of the house was not behind his desk as I'd imagined he would be. He stood facing the fireplace that barely took the chill off the air. Drafty old house. No wonder that door to the tower had swung shut.

I glanced at the portrait of Lavinia above his head and wondered if he had been addressing his dead wife. Did he miss her terribly? What had their marriage been like?

Allinson remained with his back to me, staring into the fire for a moment. I had plenty of opportunity to study his backside, the cut of the jacket that stretched across his shoulders and the length of his trouser-clad legs. The tall boots he'd worn outdoors were gone. I missed them. A pair of wingtip shoes took their place. Sir Richard was a trim, fit figure, but not the romantic paragon I'd imagined at first sight.

Then he turned to face me. My mouth went dry. The thick shock of dark hair with an errant lock or two falling over his forehead and those solemn brown eyes haunted by grief would've put Lord Byron to shame. He was indeed a poetic figure.

I cast myself as a penitent employee and dropped my gaze to the floor. "I would like to apologize for my earlier rudeness. I tend to joke when I'm nervous."

"Please sit." He gestured to one of the two chairs before the fireplace.

I took my place and waited for my scolding. Allinson strode restlessly from the fireplace to the brocade-draped window where he struck another dramatic pose, looking through the mullioned panes at the garden below.

"My sons are quite distraught from the loss of their mother last year. Their grief was so deep, I couldn't bear to send them to boarding school as scheduled. With their nanny already gone, I should have hired a caretaker, but…" He fell silent, appearing to be lost in sadness and memories.

This wasn't the reprimand I'd expected. I shifted, uncomfortably aware that my mad attraction to this man grieving the loss of his wife was wrong, not to mention pointless. Desire had hit me like a bolt from the blue, unexpected, unwanted but undeniable. Time to shake it off.

"I'm very sorry for your loss, sir. If you give me another chance, I would like to try to provide a better example for the boys. They're both bright and eager to learn. I'm certain I can prepare them to join a class of their peers by next year."

Sir Richard gave a small grunt. "Is any lad ever prepared for that battlefield?"

I'd never been to boarding school and wouldn't have offered a comment even if I had, since he clearly spoke to himself. I breathed softly, disappearing into the chair while waiting for him to make up his mind about me. I studied his classic profile, the strong nose and chin, the sharp cheekbones, the deep-set eyes under heavy brows.

"Your references and education are beyond reproach." His breath steamed the cold window glass. "Finding another likely candidate for the position might prove difficult."

His gaze finally turned to me. I sat straighter, not quite smiling since I didn't want him to think I took this lightly, but trying to appear bright and amenable and like someone who would be a positive influence on children. It was quite a juggling act.

A flicker of something I couldn't quite read passed over Allinson's eyes before he spoke again. "Very well. Prove to me your progressive methods will bear results, and I'll revisit the matter after a period of a month."

He continued to gaze at me as I registered I was being put on probation. I must prove my worth by teaching the boys something measurable, quickly.

"You may go now," Sir Richard prompted.

I leaped up from the chair. "Yes. Yes, sir. You can count on me." I bobbed my head and backed out of his presence as if he were royalty. "Thank you for this opportunity. I won't fail you."

"That remains to be seen." He stared at me even harder until it seemed impossible he wasn't looking right into my head and seeing the truth about who I was. "If you feel inclined to fall in with the savages again, I recommend you restrain yourself."

The straight line of his lips trembled slightly. Was that a smile caught in the corners? Just in case it was, I smiled back, though I continued to nod and agree. "Yes, sir."

For a mere fraction of a moment, our gazes locked as if in a silent wrestling duel. I felt the power of his presence invade me. A low throbbing in my groin coaxed my cock to stiffness. *No. Not that. Not here.*

I hurried out of the study, but those glowing eyes stayed with me. I couldn't erase Allinson's countenance from my mind. He'd been far easier on me and more forthcoming about his sons than I'd expected, while still maintaining an aura of reserve. This man of contradictions intrigued me, and I wanted to know more about him.

Not that I'd be seeing much of Sir Richard around the schoolroom.

Even a lowly slummer like me understood the aristocracy's relationship to their children was different than that of the lower classes. Children remained in their own area and interacted with their parents only once or twice a day. Nothing like the sort of household where I'd grown up, in which we all piled on top of each other in a very confined space.

When my father and three of my siblings were felled by influenza in one grand, crushing blow, my family had gotten much smaller and life became tougher and colder. Years later, my remaining sister married and moved north, taking Mum with her, and I'd remained in London with the man who'd educated me above my station. No more slums and their diseases after I evolved into Graham Cowrie.

Now I'd moved up again, from my typesetting job at the print shop to a teaching position on a grand country estate. I wouldn't jeopardize that. From here on out, I'd do what was expected with the boys and not spare so much as a lascivious thought for the master of the house—no matter how much I'd felt a flash of something earthy shooting back and forth between us.

It was time to take my role of tutor seriously and earn my way to an even better position in the future.

CHAPTER 4

By the time I returned to the schoolroom, I'd lost my students again, but Whitney and Clive had left behind pages printed in childish hand. Whit's letters were round balloons, Clive's were cramped and spidery, and the stories contained in several paragraphs were as different as the twins. They might share some elemental bond, perhaps even the ability to transmit thoughts to one another, but they were definitely two very different boys.

The corps reeched out skeltal fingers to grab the grave rober and pull him into the grave to meet his dume. The end! Whit's just desserts to a man who'd planned to steal diamonds from a dead woman ended with a jaunty flare and a very fat exclamation point.

The teecher disaperred and no one ever new what happened to him. The pupels rejoyced over tea. Clive's sinister ending warned me what might be in store for me if I remained here.

"Lovely, children." I gathered the papers and put them in a notebook. We would have to work on correcting spelling at some point, but right then, since I'd missed breakfast, I was ravenous. I'd introduce myself in the kitchen and see what I could find to eat before searching for the twins again.

This time I found my way unerringly downstairs with no detours into neglected wings of the house. On the way, I passed the maid I'd met earlier dust mopping the floor in a hallway. She looked up at my approaching footsteps then quickly bent her white-capped head again.

"By the way, I'm Graham Cowrie, the new tutor," I introduced myself, since I'd forgotten to on our first meeting.

She mopped the dark aged wood with silent intensity, refusing to acknowledge my presence.

Another standoffish, slightly odd character to win over in this godforsaken place. "You're doing a wonderful job," I added, fairly certain she'd never been complimented on her work in her entire life.

The girl darted another glance at me.

"And your name is…?" When no answer was forthcoming, just more frantic floor polishing, I moved on.

"Molly Barrett." A whisper floated after me.

"Pleased to meet you, Molly."

In the kitchen, which was three times the size of my entire flat in the city, there was more activity going on than in the rest of the house put together. A large, red-faced woman in an apron and mobcap stirred something in a pot on the enormous stove while shouting orders at a scullery maid who poured milk into glasses.

"Good morning, ladies," I greeted them. "Preparing lunch?"

The cook glared at me, and the long-jawed scullery maid gaped as if she'd seen an apparition. New additions to the staff must be a rare sight.

Cook stabbed a knife into a blob of some sort of jellied thing that sat before her on the counter. "What do you want? The young masters aren't here."

"No. I'm afraid I've misplaced the boys. *And* I've missed breakfast. Not starting off on the right foot, I'm afraid. Would you happen to have a crust of bread or spot of tea to hold me until the next meal?"

I gave her my most winning smile, but it didn't earn a simper or blush. In fact, Cook scowled all the harder. Tough audience in this house.

"We have our work to do, and you have yours. You'll eat when lunch is delivered to you—upstairs in the schoolroom with the boys. Three meals a day is all I'm required to provide."

She returned to stabbing at that poor slab of meat. I exchanged glances with the horsey-looking maid and gave an exaggerated shrug. She showed just a glimpse of a snaggletooth in a smile, shot a glance at the angry cook, and quickly returned to her work.

Such a friendly lot to spend my entire winter with, I thought as I retreated from the kitchen with a grumbling stomach.

I had no more excuse not to hunt for Whit and Clive, though I couldn't begin to guess where they were. The grounds beyond the gardens included woods, meadows, and streams. Two energetic youngsters accustomed to running wild might be anyplace. But the day had turned cloudy and rain spattered the windowpanes, so I suspected the boys might have squirreled themselves away somewhere within the enormous house.

My own sense of adventure led me to explore once more the ancient fortress at the heart of the newer wings. If I were a boy, that was where I'd spend my time. I could only assume Clive and Whit might play the same sorts of games, climbing to the highest battlements to survey the land below, imagining a legion of soldiers marching to attack the fortress, and coming up with counter strategies. Or perhaps pretending the tower was the eagle's nest of a pirate ship they captained. Either way, these flights of fancy would take place in the highest point, that grim tower. Taking into consideration the light I'd seen upon my arrival, the sound I thought I'd heard on the stairs, and the door that swung mysteriously closed, it was a good bet the boys utilized the tower as a play area.

I wended my way past many closed chamber doors and paid

another visit to the medieval chapel with its dark wooden pews and single stained glass window. A solemn aura of gravitas shrouded the room, but I found it peaceful rather than sorrowful—a completely different sensibility than that dreadful tower.

As I approached the entrance to the north tower, my logical conclusion that the twins played there began to crumble, and a sense of foreboding crept through me like early morning mist. My pace slowed, and I didn't want to take another step closer. Again a weight of hopeless despair settled on me, and I hadn't been feeling particularly melancholy until that very moment.

I inhaled and reached out to grasp the door handle. *It's just masonry. Don't be a nancy, Nancy.* I turned the handle and pulled, but the door wouldn't open. I turned and tugged again. The mechanism seemed to operate smoothly. I could only surmise the wooden door must be swollen into its frame. Very odd since it had been ajar less than an hour before.

I grabbed with both hands and pulled with all my strength. It felt almost as if the door were bolted on the other side. Perhaps the children had latched it to keep adults out of their private domain. Likely they stood on the stairwell even now, holding back their giggles at my vain attempts to breach their sanctuary.

"Whitney. Clive," I called. "Come out now. It's nearly time for lunch."

If the promise of food couldn't lure them out, I didn't know what might. The truth was I had no control over my charges and didn't know how to impose order. Sooner or later, I *would* be sacked and probably should be.

I gave one last try, hauling with all my strength, and in that moment, a feeling swept over me like an ocean wave. I wasn't fighting against a latch or a stuck door. Someone or some *thing* lurked on the other side. Not two little boys, but a powerful force blocking me from entering the tower. I felt it in the most primitive part of my being. There was something malevolent residing on the other side of that door. I let go of the metal handle as if it were hot iron and stumbled back several steps.

My mouth was so dry, I could barely gather enough moisture to speak. "Boys, enough of your games," I croaked. "I expect to see you in the schoolroom within ten minutes. Do you hear me?"

With that querulous command, I scurried away like a rat, back down the corridor, which was becoming quite familiar, and all the way to the schoolroom without pausing.

I stopped short in the doorway. Whit and Clive looked up from the table at which they sat with plates of food before them, lumps of something floating in gravy.

I caught my breath and clung to the doorway to keep my legs from crumpling. There was no way they could have reached this room ahead of me if they'd been in the tower. Not as fast as I'd run.

Perhaps some other member of the household? I tried to explain away my certainty that there'd been a presence on the other side of that door. But who, and why would anyone be there?

I couldn't shut out the persistent voice that whispered in my head, *You know it wasn't a flesh-and-blood being. You* know *it was something else.*

CHAPTER 5

I reined in my galloping imagination and shook off my superstitious apprehension. Someone had locked the door. That was all. Anyway, there were more immediate and concrete things to deal with right in front of me.

I managed to enter the room smiling. "Good day, boys. How's the meal? I see you waited for me. Good of you."

I took my place at the small table and uncovered the unappetizing-looking meal. But the smell wafting up made my stomach growl, and when I tasted a forkful, the stew was surprisingly good.

Whitney and Clive exchanged another of their looks, then both pairs of eyes settled on me, making me not the least bit self-conscious or uncomfortable.

"Did you get sacked?" Whit asked.

"Your father merely wanted to discuss your education." I chewed and swallowed another bite. "By the way, I found both of your stories very interesting, each in its own way. I hope you'll write more."

Gimlet eyes drilled into me. The boys simultaneously took another bite of food and a sip from their glasses of milk. Their unison movements were more than a little unsettling, especially since I was already on edge.

"I thought after lunch we'd have a crack at mathematics." I lowered my voice confidentially. "Not my strong suit, I must admit. Perhaps we can invent ways to make numbers more entertaining." I fired off a dazzling smile, which was met again with disappointing results—blank stares. Apparently my charm would do nothing for me here in this grim house.

All of us had apparently worked up an appetite running around outdoors earlier. In a trice, all plates were emptied and the trays set aside. It was time for me to engage my students once more. Learning times tables could be deadly dull, so I determined not to fossilize my students by making them recite the tables aloud.

The scattershot teaching method I'd invented outdoors seemed to have gained their attention, so I employed something similar. I wrote simple addition, subtraction, and multiplication problems on the chalkboard and rewarded points toward a prize to the first boy to come up with the correct answer—on paper, since Clive wouldn't speak. I was relieved that the boys' hands shot up rapidly as they raced to outdo each other.

It seemed Clive was better with numbers, or at least faster, and in the end, he won the prize—the only thing from my luggage remotely appropriate, a small bag of candies. Clive took the paper sack, opened it, and poured his booty on the table. Then he carefully split the hard candies into two piles, keeping mints for himself and pushing a smaller pile of butterscotches to his brother.

"Well done!" I approved his sharing and fished around in my mind for a way to fill the next segment of time. A movement at the door caught my attention. The footman who'd carried my luggage the previous night hovered in the doorway. Pinheaded Tommy goggled at us, then silently came in to remove the lunch trays.

"Do you like to draw?" I asked the boys. "I'll admit it's one of my favorite ways to pass the time. If you like, I can show you the technique for perspective drawing."

I passed out sheets of paper and the pens and inkwells from the supply shelf and began to demonstrate setting a horizon point and using a ruler to draw buildings receding into the distance. The boys set to work, blond heads bowed, pen nibs scratching at paper, and I turned to my own notebook, intending to jot down at least the beginning of my story in case they should ask to see it. I didn't want my ruse to get them to write to be uncovered.

Tommy still lingered over picking up the trays, a job which should've taken no more than a moment. His gaze roamed over the stark black lines the twins made on the white paper. I could see the eager interest in his eyes, as well as more intelligence than I'd suspected upon meeting him.

"You like to draw too?" I asked. "Sit down. I'll get you some paper."

I knew my offer to let him draw with the young masters was inappropriate. Tommy was a mere footman—and apparently the only one in the house from what I'd seen so far. But it could do no harm to indulge the lad in a moment's leisure. Whatever tasks he had waiting for him couldn't be that pressing: blacking shoes or polishing silver, perhaps beating the carpets. The staffing at this place seemed very strange. Shouldn't they have more than a meager handful of servants? And wasn't it unusual to hire someone like Tom in a grand house such as this?

At first, it seemed Tom would flee at my offer. He shook his head and reached for a tray. But when I laid a blank sheet of paper and another bottle of ink on the table, he sank into the chair on Whit's left and picked up the pen.

Both boys glanced at him, then returned to their own projects, which had apparently enthralled them.

I showed Tommy how to hold the pen, dip it in the ink, and draw on the paper. I wasn't going to bother with the bit about perspective, certain he couldn't grasp the concept.

"Draw whatever you like." I returned to my seat and focused on my own blank sheet, filling it with sentences about a highwayman and some buried treasure. If Clive and Whit ever read it, no doubt it would spur a bout of the twins digging into the garden beds.

When I finally glanced up, I froze with my pen nib dripping ink. Tommy's sloped head was bent over his work and a nearly architectural rendering of the Allinson estate flowed from his hand to the paper. The sketch was stunning, technically correct but also hauntingly beautiful as he'd depicted a storm of black clouds billowing over the house and grounds. His nose nearly touched the paper, and his pen flew. I watched in entranced disbelief.

At last, I realized the boys had both stopped drawing, so I turned my attention to their work. Whit's drawing was what I'd expected to see, an elemental drawing of a house-lined road receding to a set point.

Ignoring the lesson on perspective, Clive had drawn something quite different. A nightmare vision exploded across his paper. A dark, swirling, not quite human figure dominated half the page, while a small, vaguely feminine shape appeared about to be engulfed by the looming darkness. Behind her sheltering body, just outside the dark thing's grasping arms, two little figures stood hand in hand. It wasn't hard to guess they were meant to be the twins. The sense of sheer menace in the boy's drawing was undeniable.

What the *hell* had happened in this house to rob Clive of his voice and give him waking nightmares? And why didn't it seem to have affected Whit as much? Was their father meant to be the sinister monster in the drawing? I hadn't felt anything menacing, merely miserable, in Sir Richard's demeanor. But then, I'd only just met the man. I wasn't a small child living under his rule, and every family had secrets. A monster of a man had lived in my house for a time.

Tommy lifted his head, seeming to return from a trance. I complimented him on his meticulous depiction of Allinson Hall and the storm clouds that threatened it. The lad bolted from his seat, grabbed the stacked trays, and hurried from the room.

I addressed Whit and Clive. "Very good drawings, boys. Shall I pin them up on the wall?" I searched for thumbtacks in a desk drawer while continuing to talk lightly as if the nightmarish vision Clive had depicted was completely normal.

There were hours to go before teatime, and I'd already run out of ideas. I came up with the best way to pass time I could think of, reading aloud from a book of Arthurian legends. It could be considered a history lesson if one squinted and looked at it a certain way.

As the light pelting of rain on the windowpanes turned to a steady stream, I built up the fire on the hearth and settled with the boys on the carpet, pillows at our backs. They'd stopped running away from me—a good sign—and seemed content to listen to the tale of Sir Kay and his stepbrother and squire, Arthur, who, of course, pulled a certain sword from a stone to become king.

I read until I grew hoarse, asked Whit to take over. His reading was slow and halting, but no more than any other nine-year-old's might be. He stumbled over some of the more difficult words, and I asked Clive to look up the words in the dictionary. I wouldn't force him to speak, but he needed to do his share as a student.

After we'd worked our way through a couple of tales, I gave the boys leave to play for a while, suggesting they build a city from blocks.

Again they seemed quite amenable. I felt a little smug. It seemed these boys had been waiting for a kind teacher such as myself to guide them. I really was rather good at this.

I settled to work on my writing and quite lost track of time. The boys were so quiet in their play on the far side of the very large room, it was almost like being alone. The pendulum of the mantel clock ticked. Fire crackled on the hearth. Rain pattered on the casement. And I capped my pen, set my journal aside, and allowed myself to drift into a doze in the comfortable armchair.

But the dreams that filled my sleep were not comfortable at all. When I jerked awake, my heart beat quickly, and I gasped for breath as if I'd been running. I couldn't recall what I'd dreamed of, but a sense of darkness filled me, a mournful feeling of hopelessness completely at odds with my normally equitable disposition.

I shook it off and glanced over to check on the boys.

A village built with large wooden blocks, curved arches, and triangular rooftops filled the floor, but Whit and Clive were nowhere to be seen. They'd escaped again.

Did I really need to go after them? If they wanted their tea, they would return. On the other hand, I couldn't afford for them to pester the staff and someone to report to Allinson that his new tutor exercised no control.

Reluctantly, I grabbed the pair of shoes I'd taken off for comfort's sake and slid my feet into them. Rather than smooth leather, prickles and pain met my feet.

"Ouch! Damnation!"

I dragged off the shoes and upended one. Bits of thorny barberry twigs and green stuff that might have been nettle sifted from them to land on the floor. Another boyish prank from the twin imps. I cursed the boys under my breath as I cleaned up the mess and checked to make sure every bit of nature was removed from my shoes.

I'd thought I had them in the palm of my hand, that I'd created a bond with them already after only one day. But apparently it had been a temporary truce. The war was not yet over.

The rest of the day ticked by slowly. I was used to the bustle of London and the companionship of friends. This solitary existence in a quiet backwater was going to take some getting used to. How winter would drag with just me and a pair of brats getting along together. I felt sorry for myself and moped for a while. But I'm nothing if not resilient. I stiffened my upper lip, and by the time tea arrived and the twins straggled back into the room, I'd regained my composure. I behaved as if their coming and going at will did not bother me and acted as if no prickly bits had found their way into my shoes.

We ate, and after the meal, I took out a deck of cards and board and offered to teach them cribbage. As I dealt, I explained the complicated game, which should mathematically challenge a pair of young children. They'd learn statistics and quick addition in order to calculate their points. The game filled the rest of the evening, and when I called an end due to bedtime, Clive was far ahead.

CHAPTER 6

The shy maid who'd been cleaning the floor earlier came to get the boys ready for sleep. I retired to my own room for a much-needed break. But I could hear the sounds of washing up from the other room. The boys seemed surprisingly compliant.

Was I meant to tuck them in and say good night? I wasn't sure what my duties in this strange situation actually included, hired as a tutor but expected to do much more than teach. Ultimately, I chose to leave the boys in Molly's care and sat to scribble a bit more on the story I'd become quite invested in.

After I'd written for a while, I thought I'd read, but the few books I'd brought along I knew nearly by heart. Again I felt homesick for the many entertainments and friendships of my city life. Figuring the library must be extensive in a house like this, I decided to go in search of it as a distraction for my restlessness.

I walked down the hall, past the twins' quiet bedroom. The impenetrable silence in the huge house made me imagine that there was no other life there. Everyone had died or disappeared, and I was all alone. I drew my robe around me like a suit of armor that would protect me and plodded on. With a candle from my room blazing a tiny trail in the darkness, I might have slipped through a crack in time into another century.

Unsure in what direction the library might lie, I chose instead to go to the chapel, which seemed a peaceful point of refuge. As I drew near, I noticed light coming from the partially open door. I considered running back to my room, but I had to see who—or what—was inside. In the night, it was easy to believe the presence I'd felt in the tower earlier had been real, that something *other* lurked within these ancient walls.

But when I entered the chapel, a very real, solid person occupied the front pew facing the candlelit altar with its ornate iron cross. Sir Richard knelt with his head bowed, shoulders hunched, hands clasped in prayer. His posture suggested a man in deep mourning, a man begging for forgiveness or understanding from a silent god. My earlier thought that the threatening figure in Clive's drawing might possibly represent his father seemed ludicrous. Allinson was grief-stricken, not angrily violent—although it was certainly possible for one person to contain both of those emotions and more. But I couldn't believe he'd committed any sort of violence against his family.

The softer part of me that gave coins to beggars and lent rent money to unfortunate friends wanted to reach out to the man. It was my nature to try to fix things and offer comfort where I could. But I doubted Sir Richard would appreciate a servant intruding on his very vulnerable moment.

Willing my feet to be soft as cats' paws, I slowly backed out of the room. A flash of something moved in the corner of my eyes. I whipped my head toward the movement just as a tall brass candlestand fell to the stone floor with a resounding clang. This was no tabletop holder but a stand that stood nearly as tall as my shoulder. I had not brushed against it in any way. There was absolutely no reason for the heavy object to abruptly fall over like that.

But I didn't have time to ponder the mystery. My gaze shot back to Sir Richard, who had leaped up at the noise. He stared at me. I stared back, wondering whether he'd do me the kindness of letting Drover give me a ride to the train station, or if he'd put me out immediately so I had to tramp all the way to town in the dark.

The man broke from his still pose and strode toward me with such swift purpose, I instinctively took a step back.

I dove for the candlestick, intent on setting it back on its base. "Sorry. So clumsy. Didn't know anyone was in here. Thought I'd, uh, pray for guidance. I didn't mean to disturb you," I babbled.

I hauled at the brass creation with all my strength, but it was difficult to lift. Allinson grabbed hold of it, and together we set the thing upright. For a moment, we both clung to the metal, our hands only inches apart.

"I…"

Words failed me. I had no more apologies to give and couldn't have spoken them if I tried. Something very like a high-powered magnet seemed to be charging the air between us. I'd felt that attraction before, many times with many men—gazes that locked, sizzling messages shooting back and forth, the inevitable search for a place to meet in private—but I'd never felt anything as powerful as this.

Allinson's gaze was the one-two punch in the final round of a boxing match. It hit me in the solar plexus, driving the breath from me and leaving me stunned.

"I…" It came out a whisper the second time. I stopped myself from grabbing my employer and hauling him to me, and forced out another word. "Sorry. Won't happen again."

I unstuck my fingers from the candlestand and backed away.

Sir Richard blinked. His jaw tightened before he replied. "See that it doesn't. Stay in your own area, Mr. Cowrie. The estate isn't yours to explore."

"No," I agreed. "But it *is* rather like a museum. I can't help being interested in the history of the place. Is there a book or a family history of the place? I was hoping to use your library, if I that's all right. I was trying to find my way there, but got turned around."

Sir Richard's eyes widened, perhaps in surprise that I continued to jabber after his clear message to get out of his sight. His lips compressed for a moment but then he said, "I suppose that would be all right. I'll show you the way."

He extinguished the candles on the altar, the glow bathing the stark planes of his face as he puffed on each one. Couldn't help thinking I'd like to have those slightly pursed lips pressed against mine. I knew almost for certain my instinct about his inclinations wasn't wrong, despite his grieving over a dead wife. I had enough experience to recognize a fellow man lover when I met one. But I filed my attraction under "not to be opened until the twelfth of never" as I followed him and his lamp out of the room and down the hallway.

Several twists and turns and a stairway or two brought us to our destination. It turned out the grand library was only across the hall from Allinson's study. And it *was* a grand room lined to the ceiling with books, most of which looked as if they hadn't been cracked open in years. My fingers itched to get at them, blow the dust off those pages. Even if many of the old books were boring as mud, there must be some hidden gems among them.

Sir Richard stood silently off to my left. It took me a moment to pull myself from my examination of the room enough to be aware that he was watching me. "You love books."

"Always have loved stories. When I was young, I didn't have access to many books." I bit the tip of my tongue as I recalled I was supposed to be a gentleman fallen on hard times. It wouldn't do to reveal my hardscrabble background. I must remember my invented persona at all times, never let the mask slip.

"In your letter applying for the post, you mentioned your family had been stricken with debt. Who paid for your university education?"

"An uncle, now dead."

In fact, I'd had no formal education but had read a number of books recommended by my patron, Sylvester Leighton. Later, a drunken former university professor who lived in my building had been overjoyed to pour his fount of knowledge over me. The old man had truly loved teaching before he got the boot. I'd had access to his brain and his books. It was a portion of his legacy upon his death that occupied the trunk in my room.

Sir Richard's questioning made me nervous. Did he suspect something was off about me? Did he pry to get at the truth? Or was my own guilt making me suspicious of an innocent question? At any rate, I wanted to change the subject from me to anything else.

"Perhaps you could recommend a favorite book," I suggested. "I'd value your opinion."

The question was enough to take Allinson's relentless gaze off me, which was a relief. He led the way to a bookcase near the large fireplace dominating one end of the room. The book spines there appeared newer and shinier. I half expected him to pull out a volume of Dante's *Inferno*. It seemed the sort of dark fare he might wallow in. I was pleasantly surprised when he withdrew a slim blue book and placed it in my hands.

"*The Adventures of Sherlock Holmes.*" I read the title aloud, as if proving to the man I had the ability. "A new Conan Doyle book! I didn't know he'd published another."

"Brand-new. I picked it up in London on my last visit. Fodder for the masses, to be sure, but I'll admit to enjoying these detective tales." Richard's well-bred drawl reminded me that gentlemen such as he were expected only to admire the classics and not more plebian adventure tales.

I leafed through the pages, as excited as a boy on Christmas morning. "*The Sign of Four* was a thrilling tale. *A Study in Scarlet* less so, in my opinion."

"Agreed," Allinson said, and for the first time, I felt as if I were carrying on a conversation with one of my mates rather than an intimidating superior. "As well as providing more insight into Holmes's character, which makes him more believable."

I studied the table of contents. "Which case is the best, or do I need to read them in order?"

Allinson stood near me to read over my shoulder. He smelled of pipe smoke and soap and his liquor-scented breath wafted to my nose when he replied. "No particular reading order is necessary. 'The Adventure of the Copper Beeches' contains quite an intriguing mystery."

"Excellent. The last shall be first, then." I closed the book and turned to my employer with a smile—which quickly died on my lips. He stood so close, I swore I could feel his heart beating. The evening stubble on his jaw and upper lip and his disheveled clothes made him seem more human, less like the domineering gentleman I'd met earlier that day. Our gazes met in the dim, intimate room, and any one of a number of things might happen if we so chose.

Not a good idea, I reminded myself.

At the same moment, Sir Richard moved to face the fireplace, as if to warm himself before the nonexistent fire on the hearth.

"Thank you for the loan of the book. I shall probably stay up half the night reading it." I held the book in front of my chest like a breastplate for my robe armor. Realizing this made me sound irresponsible, I added,

"But I shall be certain to rise at the crack of dawn along with Whit and Clive."

Sir Richard's head snapped around. "What did you call him?"

I scrabbled around in my mind for what he meant. "Um…Whit? Whitney seemed too large a name for such a small boy." I cleared my throat. "I'm sorry. If you don't approve of nicknames, I shan't shorten it again."

He waved a hand, brushing away the apology. "No. It's just… I never called him Whit, but his mother did."

"Oh." I didn't know what to say about that. The boy hadn't shown any sign of emotion when I used the affectionate version of his name, but it certainly seemed to affect Richard mightily. "I'll stop, then."

He shook his head and said shortly, "Call him what you will. It simply took me by surprise. Enjoy the book."

He turned from me, dismissing me.

I padded out of the room in my slippers, which were too thin in the soles to keep the chill from the stone floors at bay. Living in the remains of a castle might sound romantic but was actually quite uncomfortable.

Even though I was hardly paying attention to directions, I found my way back to my room without getting lost. If I'd been restless before venturing out of my room, my mind was abuzz with energy now. I replayed every second of my time with the master of the house, recalled the details of his face and form, the tenor of his voice, and rejoiced that we both liked mysteries. Of course, I'd never admit to him I also enjoyed penny dreadfuls, the lurid tales from which I'd learned to read. The thrills and chills of pulp magazines were a step down from Conan Doyle's more sophisticated Holmes stories, which were also considered low-brow reading by the well-educated.

It seemed with mysteries, Sir Richard and I actually had something in common, other than a perverse attraction to each other we would never give voice to.

I jumped under many layers of covers, planning to create a pocket of warmth and dive into one of the Holmes mysteries. But the very long day filled with new characters and strange experiences caught up with me. I fell asleep without turning down the wick of my lamp, and when I awoke, the oil was gone and sunlight streamed through the windowpanes.

CHAPTER 7

The next day, I remained dutifully in the schoolroom with the boys as their father had directed for as long as I could stand it. I managed to keep their interest in simple mathematics by pretending their toys were items on a store's shelves and giving the boys their own hand-crafted currency to purchase with. A read-aloud period was followed by a penmanship lesson in which I had them write words from the story. But by early afternoon, I was as restless as the boys, eager to be outdoors on such a fine day.

"Let's explore nature and identify the specimens of flora and fauna we discover," I suggested.

We all pulled on Wellington boots to march through the mud the previous day's rain had left behind and escape the oppressive gloom of the house. Once outside with the sun on my face and the breeze in my hair, my gloomy spirit almost immediately lifted.

Things were going quite well, actually. At least my young charges hadn't run away from me today and seemed quite willing to go along with whatever I suggested. No more prickly things in my shoes or bed so far that day either. Perhaps they were enjoying my company a little.

We sloshed around in a boggy area near a stream at the far east corner of the field where we'd played the day before. Whit collected various leaves, and I helped him identify them with the botany book I'd brought along. Clive came over with a crayfish in hand, its tiny claws clicking as it squirmed, trying to free itself. The boy was muddy and damp all over, but for the first time, he almost smiled.

Whit and I admired his catch for several minutes.

"Very interesting, but since we have no place to keep him, I think you'll have to let the crayfish go."

Clive's perpetual frown returned.

"The little creature wouldn't be happy in a jar or even an aquarium," I pointed out. "Wild things are best left to live their lives as nature intended."

Clive looked from the crayfish to me, searching my face before nodding slightly. I felt quite triumphant. For the first time, we'd communicated directly without Clive using Whit to speak for him. He set the crayfish down, and we all watched it scuttle away and disappear into its burrow in the mud.

We spent hours mucking about by the creek, until hunger eventually drove us to return to the confines of the house. Late in the day, wet, filthy, and contented, we tramped across the field. The looming hulk of Allinson Hall blocked the sun as we approached. When we entered the building's shadow, nerves tingled along my spine and an inexplicable melancholy invaded my sunny disposition. I had a propensity for the dramatic, but this didn't feel like anything my imagination had conjured. Sadness flooded through me like a palpable and externally inflicted mood—something beyond my control.

I hustled the boys through one of the back entrances, determined to avoid contact with anyone before we'd gotten cleaned up.

Smart enough to understand the need for secrecy, Whit led the way to a narrow staircase behind a closed door, a route taken by servants in years past to move about the house unseen by the nobility, but it was evidently no longer in use. I sneezed on the dust and cobwebs caught in my hair as I followed the boys up.

We emerged not far from my bedroom. I recalled the whispers and footsteps from my first night in the house and guessed this was where the boys had hidden after sabotaging my bed.

After washing and changing, we met again in the schoolroom, where our tea trays awaited us at the table. Stone-cold soup had turned to an unpalatable gel. But we devoured it anyway, along with the rest of our meals and the room-temperature glasses of milk. Before we'd quite finished, a shadow fell in the doorway. Tom had arrived to take away the trays.

The lad slunk into the room, head hanging. If he were a dog, I'd think his master had whipped him. I wondered if someone in this house had done something similar.

"Hello, Tom," I greeted him, and Whitney followed my example. Clive remained mute.

Tommy lingered over the task of collecting the remains of our meal, and it occurred to me he was hoping for a repeat of yesterday's art lesson.

I obliged him by suggesting to the boys they draw illustrations to go with the short stories they'd written the previous day.

"Would you like some paper too?" I asked Tom. Moments later, all three boys were gathered around the table, applying charcoal pencils to paper.

I'd earned a break and took the opportunity to dive into the mystery Allinson had suggested. Soon my mind was filled with the story of secret identity and a locked wing of an ancient house, which rang far too familiar given my current living situation.

I was so wrapped up in the suspenseful climax of "The Copper

Beeches," I jerked when an unexpected voice intruded on the story.

"Tommy Smith. So this is where you've been hiding yourself this past hour!" Mrs. Growler stood near the doorway, hands on hips. The housekeeper appeared as large and surly as when I'd first met her. Did no one in this godforsaken place own a smile?

Poor Tom bolted up from the table, dropping his pencil on his half-finished sketch.

Mrs. Growler pointed her finger like a skewer. "Get back to your duties, you oafish lout, lest you find yourself out of a job."

Tom clattered the trays and dishes together in his hurry to obey. I was determined to alleviate the scolding and punishment he might receive.

"Most of the blame is mine, Mrs. Growler. I invited the lad to join us. He has quite an artistic bent." I snatched up Tom's picture and showed it to her.

She glanced and grunted. "You should know better, Mr. Cowrie. 'Tis most inappropriate, not to mention inconvenient, for Tom to fall behind on his work. Don't let it happen again."

Tom might be as mute as Clive, for all I could tell. I hadn't yet heard him speak a word. But his eyes communicated volumes of dismay as the housekeeper made this pronouncement.

"What about later in the evenings? Would it be all right for Tom to come to the schoolroom for an art lesson?" As if I, who had the drawing skills of a three-legged dog, might teach this young man anything. But I could provide him with the materials to indulge his creativity.

Mrs. Growler scowled some more. "He couldn't use the children's supplies. That wouldn't be right."

"No, of course not, but I have some paper and ink of my own I could let him use." I twinkled my dimples at her, a habit I might as well break since it got me nowhere with these hard-nosed northerners. If anything, my attempt at charm seemed to sway Mrs. Growler more toward saying no. She clicked her tongue and rolled her eyes before finally capitulating.

"An hour now and again in the evening will surely do no harm. Lord knows the lad has little enough joy in his life."

Did I detect a sensitive chink in her grim façade? Perhaps Mrs. Growler wasn't such a termagant after all. Then she clapped her hands together, loud enough to make me and all three boys jump. "Come now, Tom. Back to work."

After the servants had gone, it was just me and the twins again, me and two restless children whose attention was ready to be directed toward something new. Teacher, caretaker, nursemaid, I was already worn out from the responsibility. And this was only my second day! What would it be like as winter shut us all indoors for days on end and there was no respite from sheer boredom?

I gazed back at the two expectant faces watching me, and for a moment, I thought I might flee. I almost wished Sir Richard had sacked me so the decision would have been taken out of my hands. I could return to London and beg for my job back. My digs weren't great, and typesetting was boring, but at least I'd have all my free time to myself. I'd have my friends and occasional dalliances, theaters, museums, pubs, restaurants, all the city had to offer. I'd managed to entertain myself despite low income for most of my life. Was it really worth being in this horrible backwater simply to try to move up in the world? And what place would I reach? A similar isolated position teaching children? I doubted I had the temperament for it in the long run.

"Tell us your story." Whit interrupted my thoughts. "What's it about?"

Ah yes, the story I'd promised in order to get them to write one for me. I'd only scribbled a start, but as long as the boys didn't ask to read it, I could extemporize.

"All right. It's a mystery concerning a highwayman called Bloody Bones. Are you certain you won't be too frightened?"

Two heads shook in unison and four blue eyes riveted on me like bright tacks.

"If you're certain. I don't want anyone having nightmares later."

"We won't. Nothing scares us. Not after..." Whit cut himself short, and Clive jabbed him in the side with an elbow.

Now *that* was interesting. I wanted to press for more information, but any fool knows asking a child questions only makes them close up like little clam shells. I'd have to weasel my way into Whit's confidence.

"Very well, then. I can see you're two quite grown-up lads, ready to hear even the most vile and gory of stories. Harken, then, to the tale of *Bloody Bones and the Nightmare Hearse.*"

I put on my best recitation voice and began the story, which had percolated in my mind for some time. I'd planned to write and submit to one of the pulp magazines but somehow never found the time. Fear of not being good enough to be accepted even by the cheapest rag kept me from starting the project. But now I'd jotted down a beginning at last, I found I enjoyed writing, and my story was certainly no worse than the sensational drivel I'd read in the penny dreadfuls.

The boys sat at the table, chins resting on their arms, listening intently. It didn't take long for me to tell the part I'd already written and begin freely spinning the tale to its dramatic conclusion. By the time I reached the climax in which the highwayman with the heart of gold rushes to outrace the devil's hearse and save the fair maiden from her deadly fate, I was on my feet, describing the action with hands as well as voice. When the round-eyed boys appeared a little too caught up in the scary chase, I mimicked riding a horse, which made them both laugh.

Just as the chase reached a fever pitch, with Bloody Bones forced off the road and crossing a gully, I glanced up to see a more frightening sight than the devil himself standing in the schoolroom door.

Sir Richard leaned against the frame, arms crossed. His dark hair was windblown and his face flushed. Coupled with the breeches and tall boots, his appearance suggested he'd just been riding.

I faltered, forgetting my place in the story, and the boys looked to see what had caught my attention. Their reaction was like two turtles snapping heads and limbs back inside their shells. The giggles died in their throats, and their expressions smoothed into blankness. They got up from their chairs as if ready to sidle away, but there was no place to go since their father stood in the doorway.

For a moment, we all remained in tableau, unable to move or speak. Then Sir Richard inclined his head. "Go on. Finish the story."

I could hardly deny my employer's direct request, but my tale limped to a rather pathetic conclusion. My heart was no longer in the telling of how the highwayman outwitted the devil and won the heart of the lady far above his station. Nor did I have the attention of my audience. The boys shifted from foot to foot, obviously uncomfortable in their father's presence. Why did they seem to fear him so? I couldn't help but resurrect my first guess that he had hurt or threatened them in some way. But I could hardly reconcile that with my other impressions of him. When he'd said he couldn't bear to send his sons to boarding school while they still mourned the loss of their mother, I'd been convinced he cared.

Now he cast his gaze on one boy, then the other. "Whitney. Clive. I hope you're behaving well for Mr. Cowrie."

Neither answered, shuffling their feet and gazing down at the carpet.

"Please go to your room for a moment. I'd like a word with your teacher."

"Yes, sir," Whit mumbled.

Sir Richard entered the room, and his sons skirted around him as if he had the plague before disappearing out the door. I braced myself for the tongue-lashing I'd earned for telling horror tales rather than teaching Latin.

There we were again, two men alone in a very quiet room. My heart pounded in my ears. It was an odd sensation, caught halfway between fear and outrageous temptation. Allinson had the power to dismiss me, but I had some power over him too. I could see it in the widening of his eyes and the flare of his nostrils as he drew near. There was something silent yet undeniable between us.

"I interrupted your story," he said at last.

"The boys worked hard on lessons today, and I thought they'd earned some entertainment. Just a little tale I concocted."

"A very spooky one, from the sound of it." He wandered over to the wall where the boys' drawings were tacked and bent to study each one.

"As a boy, I liked nothing better than a chilling story. I guessed Clive and Whit…ney would feel the same." I watched the tall, handsome man prowl the room. He paused to trace a finger over the womanly shape facing off against the black, threatening presence in Clive's drawing.

"Given their mother's death, dwelling on the otherworldly and bizarre hardly seems wise," Allinson said.

"Perhaps not. I didn't really think…" I trailed off. "But it seems such worries are already in their minds. A very wise man I once knew believed that expressing one's fears through the arts was a healthy way to dispel them."

He looked at me. "Your father?"

I shook my head. "No. My father died when I was quite young.

This was…a friend." More than a friend. Sylvester Leighton had been lover, mentor, paternal figure, and more, for several very crucial years of my life.

Allinson resumed studying the drawings, moving on to Tom's portrait of the house. "Fathers and sons are often at odds. My own sons…" He paused for a long moment. "My boys have not been the same since Lavinia's death. I confess I don't know how to reach out to them. I believe they blame me…"

As if realizing he'd offered too much personal information to a servant, Allinson abruptly straightened and started toward the door. "Carry on as you have been. Teach them indoors or out as you see fit. I haven't heard either of my sons laugh in months. Today, as I approached this room, their laughter echoed down the hallway. I was happy to hear it."

He didn't look at me as he spoke, but I accepted the compliment all the same.

"They're very bright, high-spirited boys," I responded. "I'm pleased to be teaching them." And I realized that I was. Despite growing tired of having to invent and engage and entertain, I *did* enjoy working with Whit and odd little Clive.

I wanted to talk further with Sir Richard, to point out, in case he'd missed it, that one of his boys refused to speak a word, that both of them needed him to give them more attention and maybe put an arm around them once in a while, that he definitely needed to get to the root of why they might blame him for their mother's death. But none of this was my business to discuss. I was merely a servant. The most I could do was teach the boys to the best of my ability.

Allinson paused in the doorway. "Did you read 'The Copper Beeches' mystery?"

"Nearly finished. I'm enjoying it very much. Thank you for the loan of the book."

He dipped his head in acknowledgment and then, as shy and standoffish as Clive, he slipped away.

I released a breath, and my hammering heart began to slow. Oh, the effect that man had on me, and how I wished something could come of it.

I began to tidy the room. Intending to add the boys' new artwork to the wall, I gathered their drawings. When I actually took a look at Tom's, I gasped.

Again he'd drawn the house, but this time the tower filled the page. The stone walls were etched with precision, and the conical roof appeared exactly as it was in reality. But what seized my attention was one of several windows high in the tower. Tom had drawn a face, a woman's pale face against an obsidian blackness, tiny yet so detailed, I could *feel* her emotion.

The woman's eyes were wide, and her mouth was open in a silent scream.

CHAPTER 8

I needed to know more about Lavinia Allinson, dead wife and mother. Who was she, and what were the circumstances of her death? Why did the boys seem to hold their father accountable? Did he truly have some hand in her death, or was it mere childish blame for a loss they couldn't comprehend?

If so, I understood that feeling. After my father, infant brother, and two sisters died, I'd been illogically angry with my mum, as if she should have done something to save them. Weren't adults supposed to be all-powerful and protect their children, even defying death itself? It had taken me a bit of time to shake off such foolishness, and then Mum had given me a real reason to resent her by bringing Roger Dwyer into our lives.

I considered who in this odd household might be willing to talk to me about the Allinson family. I finally decided my best bet might be Smithers.

One afternoon, I stopped by the boys' room to tell them to read for a while, only to find both sprawled across their beds, sleeping like cherubs. An earlier tramp through nature that day had worn them out.

Downstairs, I wandered through several rooms, admiring paintings, antique furniture, ornate lamps, and family heirlooms. I stopped to study a portrait of some long-dead Allinson whose handsome features remained alive in Sir Richard. Put the master of the house in a ruff and cape and he could pass for his ancestor.

"May I help you?" Smithers's unexpected voice came from behind me.

I turned to face his unblinking gaze. "Actually, I was searching for you. I wanted to ask a few questions." He didn't reply, so I forged ahead. "I'm rather adrift here. I feel as if I've walked into the middle of a play and don't know all the characters or what has transpired. It would help if I knew more of the circumstances surrounding Lavinia Allinson's death. I know nothing other than that she has passed."

"The circumstances need not concern you, nor should they affect your ability to impart knowledge to the young masters."

How did he talk without moving any facial muscles except his lips? Extraordinary.

"I don't mean to pry or indulge in idle gossip. My first responsibility is to the twins, and I feel I can best reach them if I understand more about their loss."

The man blinked slowly. "Next month will be the anniversary. Mrs. Allinson died from a sudden fever. If you have further questions, I suggest you ask them of the master."

He stepped aside, making it clear I should vacate the room. I walked past him, feeling his eerie presence behind me, and continued on toward the rear of the house, thinking I'd take another quick walk before dealing with the boys again.

When I turned to say as much to Smithers, the butler had vanished.

"Sneaky as a cat," I muttered.

It was a little too chilly to be outdoors without a coat, but I couldn't bear to return to the house. Once inside, I might not be able to escape again. So I strode quickly down one garden path then another to get my blood rushing, and surveyed the detritus of the summer's growth. Soon those crunchy stalks and flowers gone to seed would melt back into the earth. Barren winter would hold sway for many months of drenching rain and occasional spitting snow, and always the rushing wind over this barren northern land.

On my left, I passed an overgrown yew hedge. Curious to see what the garden on the other side might be like, I walked the perimeter but found no entrance. The hedge was far too dense to infiltrate, with no bare spots through which I might peer at the other side. I stepped back and studied the uninterrupted wall of green.

My whim became a mission. I *would* find my way to the other side. I'd always felt obstacles were made to be overcome.

The quiet murmur of someone speaking on the far side of the hedge caught my attention. I held my breath and listened more intently, but the moment I focused on it, the soft whisper ceased. Was someone or several people inside the garden? Perhaps it was a clandestine meeting place for lovers? I grinned at the idea of scrawny Smithers and behemoth Mrs. Growler indulging in a forbidden affair. That was something I must see.

Of course, I didn't really believe they were the couple. Maybe that little maid Molly and some footman or stable lad I hadn't yet met. Certainly not Tom. That was beyond even my imagination.

I walked the hedge more slowly this time. The voice seemed to come and go intermittently, never loud enough for me to be certain I'd actually heard anything. I had a growing sense the disembodied voice wasn't a living person but an audible remnant of something long past.

A few of my London friends practiced spiritualism. I'd participated in some of their séances and half believed—all right, maybe more than *half*—that the dead moved around us, unseen and unheard until they manifested to someone receptive enough to be aware of them. I'd never been a "sensitive" such as my pseudo-medium friend Madame Alijeva described, but supposedly even the most committed skeptics occasionally had an encounter. Given what I'd experienced since arriving at Allinson Hall, I could well believe in otherworldly entities existing here.

As if bolstered by my faith, the murmuring voice seemed to gather strength, though still not sufficient for me to make out words. At the same moment, I spied a narrow gap in the hedge. I pushed aside a swath of branches that had hidden it and wedged my body through the hole, scraping my face and hands on twigs. If this had once been the true entrance to the garden, no one had used it in quite some time.

When I scanned the hidden garden, I wasn't surprised to see no one there. I rubbed at a scratch on my cheek and picked leaves from my hair as I turned in a slow circle. The flower beds were as untended as in the other gardens. A rose bed become a tangle of thorns graced the center of the rectangular space with a dry fountain as its centerpiece. A goat-legged satyr played his Pan flute. The basin below him held green slime-coated water and a spill of dead leaves.

Stone-paved paths had been devoured by grass and knee-high weeds. I trudged through them to examine a stone grotto across the garden. This six-foot-tall alcove held the marble statue of an angel with her arms outstretched in blessing.

I stopped in front of the statue, grimed with dirt and moss and missing one hand and the tip of her nose. She stood on a base as tall as my waist. Arranged around her feet was a pool of blue satin—a woman's gown, an altar cloth of sorts. Only the statue's white feet gleamed in the dimness. Polished by small hands, I realized as I noticed the camp inside the grotto.

A soggy rug covered the ground between the angel's base and the stone wall. Several mildewed pillows rested on it as well as a blanket and a rusty tin box. Boyishly crafted rifles made of slabs of wood, a slingshot, a dilapidated stuffed bear, also soggy from the recent rain.

Careful to disturb nothing, I squatted to open the box with the broken lock. Inside were normal boyhood treasures, jacks and a ball, a couple of miniature lead soldiers, toy horses. There was also a folded sheet of paper, well worn at the creases. Convincing myself it wasn't prying and I needed to learn more about my charges, I unfolded the paper to read the boys' secret thoughts.

We somenly vow to avenge Mothers death.

Sincrly,

The twins' carefully written names were followed by two brown-red fingerprints. A blood pact. Did they truly believe their father was somehow accountable?

Was he? Why did the circumstances surrounding Lavinia Allinson's death seem shrouded in mystery? A *sudden fever* seemed far too vague an explanation. I must uncover the heart of it and whether there was another side to Sir Richard, one darker and more sinister than I believed him capable of.

I replaced the box and left the boys' camp. No—their refuge, notable for the fact that it was outside the house.

As a youth, I'd had someplace similar to retreat to when things grew rough at home. After my father died, Mum grasped on to brutish, hard-handed Roger Dwyer, who controlled our house with an iron fist. I'd escaped at every opportunity, hiding in my burrow in a nearby cemetery, sleeping in one of the older crypts with easily broken hinges. For the two years Dwyer ruled our house, this was my private space. I'd only slink home occasionally to see if my mum or Cynthia, needed anything. I invited Cynthia to join me if ever Dwyer laid a hand to her, but my older sister had her own escape. His name was Johnny Carlson, and she married him at age fifteen. Later, when they moved from London, they took my mum along.

Now, as I wandered the overgrown paths in the secret garden, I recalled that terrible period in my life. I'd locked it away for quite some time, since it meant nothing in my adult life. I could look back now and feel sympathy for the youth who'd found a cemetery less frightening than home. I'd had quite a tutorial watching from my little den as men coupled in one of the few secret meeting spots available to them in the city. It was a common practice for working-class Joes to meet rich men with coins to spare for a little pleasure.

This practice I participated in myself when I grew a bit older. I became so accustomed to observing men sucking and fucking, I nearly forgot society in general didn't hold with it and we could be prosecuted for our perversion. The act never seemed wrong to me, no more than Sallys-in-the-alleys who lifted their skirts for customers with far less fear of coppers. I probably would've eventually gotten nabbed down on my knees in front of some bloke if Sylvester Leighton hadn't taken my life in an entirely different direction. Now I'd diverted my life onto yet another path, one that had proven stranger than expected, I thought as I headed back to the gap in the hedge.

"Good-bye, Mrs. Allinson or ghost of some long-dead lady-in-waiting," I said to the garden before climbing through the opening.

I headed toward the house in that golden time before twilight. The sun wasn't quite setting, but the land was gilded in late-afternoon light. I had a view of the wilder lands beyond the garden stretching to the horizon, vast stretches of land that made a city man like myself, used to enclosing buildings, uneasy.

I spotted a mounted figure thundering across the landscape. Bareheaded, dark coat flapping behind him, erect in the saddle as a general leading men into battle. The dark rider blended into his black horse so I could hardly tell where one ended and the other began. Sir Richard—it could be no one else—was a thrilling sight to behold and a figure straight from my romantic fantasies. I couldn't easily put him out of my mind or ignore my attraction, when every time I turned around he seemed to be right in front of me.

Was I growing rock hard and shaky-kneed for a man who'd done something awful to his wife and who terrorized his sons? Was I as bad as my weak-willed mother, who'd been so charmed by a vile man and so afraid of being alone she'd put up with anything to remain with him? If Roger Dwyer hadn't gotten beaten to death in a street brawl, she probably never would've been free of the man.

Not such a fool as that. I could separate my primal desire for Allinson from a clear-headed investigation into whether he was a murderer—not that I actually expected to discover he was. No messy feelings would cloud my judgment. I was Graham Cowrie, tutor extraordinaire and now Sherlock Holmes of the north.

CHAPTER 9

It was difficult to uncover facts when there was no one to talk to except two young boys, whom I could hardly grill about the circumstances surrounding their mother's death. I didn't mind my time with Clive and Whit. Although they weren't the easiest children to grow fond of, we got along all right. I grew quite invested in the challenge of creating new ways to keep their busy minds occupied.

We soon fell into a routine of sorts, starting our days with lessons best learned by rote, such as the times table, then moving on to history. When they went to boarding school, the boys would be expected to know the dates of some major events, but I tried to bring history alive with the more personal stories of the people involved. Anything told as a story became instantly more memorable.

Sometimes I'd call on the boys to help me act out a scene. This was tricky since Clive could deliver no lines. But he *was* good at swordplay, and I'd often allow them to play under the guise of learning. Active children are happy children—or as happy as these two odd ducks could be.

By midmorning we—meaning I—were ready for a break. Unless it was pouring buckets, we'd trudge across the wild lands or play tag in the gardens. I never let on that I'd found their secret hideout. The walled garden belonged to the boys alone.

Back in the schoolroom, we'd devour our lunch, then relax over an art project or craft before beginning afternoon classes.

I caught not a glimpse of Sir Richard, who never sent for the boys to be brought to him in the evenings. I'd learned from Sylvester Leighton that was the way of the wealthy, a daily cursory acknowledgment of their offspring. Allinson didn't seem to care even that much. His neglect made my opinion of him shift more to the negative side. But for all I knew, he'd left the estate again. Certainly no one would keep me informed of his comings and goings.

As days passed, I experienced no more intimations of an invisible presence, movements at the edge of my sight, mysterious whispers, or those dark moods that had overcome me just after my arrival. But I also kept myself as far from the older parts of the building, including the tower, as possible.

Tom came to me each evening for his lessons, which consisted of him drawing or painting with great talent and me occasionally watching but mostly working on my story. I'd questioned Tom about the woman in the tower, but he wouldn't say who the drawing was meant to depict. I learned he could talk, but his vocabulary was limited, and he expressed more through his drawings than with words.

Sometimes Tom drew landscapes, evocative depictions that placed one right inside the scene. Other times he drew animals so lifelike, one felt if he touched the paper, he would feel fur. Occasionally he painted or drew the Hall or the boys, and those were always dark and foreboding works, with black washes of ink or paint suggesting awful things hidden in the shadows.

One evening I rested my hand on his shoulder and studied his drawing. It was of Tom standing behind Clive and Whit as though keeping watch over them.

"What is it, Tom? What haunts this place?" I whispered.

He looked up at me, his eyes brighter and more intelligent than I'd ever guessed they could be under that sloping brow. His big jaw worked as if he wanted to say something but fought to hold it back. Forehead creasing in a frown, he shook his head before emitting one word. "Evil."

It was all I could get out of him, and it was only enough to make me more anxious and concerned. Were my two young charges in any real danger? Surely not from some incorporeal entity, but perhaps from something or someone else.

By the end of my second week of teaching, I was so suspicious and so desperate for adult companionship, I came close to searching out Smithers to talk to, but I knew a quest for conversation with him would be futile.

I went down to the servants' hall at dinner one day, intent on meeting the rest of the invisible staff, only to find that I'd already encountered them all. The long table, which once must've held more than a dozen staff members, now seated only Smithers, Growler, Cook, Tom, Molly the maid, and the unnamed scullery maid. They all stared at me with the welcoming manner of shipwreck survivors assessing a stranger who threatened their food supply.

"Good evening. Although it seems I've met most of you, I thought I'd formally introduce myself. I'm Graham Cowrie. I've looked forward to meeting you all, but it seems our paths would never cross unless I made the effort." I babbled nervously and smiled too widely.

Smithers gestured me to a chair, and the cook's helper jumped up to get a table setting for me. She set the plate and cutlery in front of me while seemingly trying not to get too close. Did she think I'd grab her and eat her for dinner?

It was all too strange, and the rest of my meal with the staff didn't get any better. I tried several conversational gambits that were met with desultory answers or silence. Eating in silence is *not* conducive to good digestion, despite what vow-taking monks might claim. Uncomfortable and awkward were only two of the adjectives I could apply to the situation. The rest were curses unfit to write down.

At last, since things could get no worse, I bluntly brought up what had bothered me since I arrived at this weird place. "This seems a small number to tend such a large house."

Molly and the scullery maid exchanged a look but seemed afraid to speak lest they earn the housekeeper's disapproval.

Mrs. Growler, she of the Amazonian stature and disposition, refolded her napkin. "Sir Richard is often away and never entertains. Our staff is sufficient to care for the portion of the house in use."

I pictured the many shut-up rooms with furniture shrouded in sheets. "What about when Mrs. Allinson was alive? Did the family entertain then? Was there more activity?"

Molly gasped audibly, as if I'd cursed aloud. The girl had information. I was determined I'd get her alone some time and wheedle it out of her.

"That is not your concern," Smithers repeated his favorite refrain. "I suggest, Mr. Cowrie, you focus on the duties you've been hired to do and spend less time questioning how things are run here."

The part of me that still relived the days when Roger Dwyer had bullied me and would no longer put up with being cowed took over use of my voice. I knew I'd probably get no answers to any of my questions, but I was agitated from two weeks of isolation, so I blurted some of them anyway.

"I live here now, Mr. Smithers. I believe I have the right to understand how things are done. For instance, does anyone work in the stable other than the coachman who picked me up at the station? Who does the laundry? Molly, here? Does the store in the village deliver supplies? And is the master of the house currently in residence or traveling again?" This was like tossing a stone into thick, brackish water where it caused no ripples. I expected no response.

Mrs. Growler gave me the gimlet eye but, surprisingly, answered. "A washerwoman from the village collects the laundry once a week. Day maids are occasionally hired as needed. Perishables are delivered directly by local farmers. Other items come by train from the city and are delivered from the village. Sir Richard is currently at home and busy running the estate." Her sharp gaze filleted me better than Cook had done the fish on my plate. "Are all of your questions answered, Mr. Cowrie?"

"Yes. I, um… That explains some things." Of course I hadn't dared to ask my biggest question of all—what had happened to Mrs. Allinson that the mere mention of her name caused Molly to gasp? Were mysterious circumstances surrounding her death merely a figment of my overactive imagination, or had something occurred?

I limped through the rest of that meal, hobbled by Mrs. Growler's chastening tongue, then beat a retreat back up to my own domain. The schoolroom and my bedroom were beginning to feel like a little safe island in a turbulent sea. I spent the evening playing cards with the boys, and, for the rest of that week, I awaited my first day off with the eagerness of a child anticipating Christmas.

When the morning finally arrived, I barely said good-bye to the twins before breaking free of the manor house and hurrying to the stable. I'd chatted with Mr. Drover a few days before, and he'd promised to take me to the village as he was set to pick up a few things. I was glad, because the long walk would've taken up most of my precious morning.

As the wagon creaked over the rutted road, I was reminded how very isolated the Allinson estate was. "Mr. Drover, can you tell me a little about the estate's history and such?"

"The house been there many a year," he offered.

I waited, but apparently Drover was as taciturn as every other person in the vicinity. Maybe it was a trait of northerners.

"When did the Allinsons first come to own it?"

"Ahh…" More silence followed. "It's belonged to the family many a year. The land was bestowed by some king, to the best of my recollection."

"Has the family lost its fortune? It seems the place is understaffed, and the building is…quite worn." A crumbling monstrosity was closer to the truth.

His shaggy brows drew into a ponderous frown, and he slowly shook his head. "No. I don't believe so. The farms and mill never done better. Prosperous years around here, these past few."

So where did the money go? Was Sir Richard a gambler who lost his fortune at gaming tables in the city? I didn't see him as the type. For one thing, it would've required him being rather social, and he seemed to prefer solitude. Perhaps his neglect of the house, like that of his children, was simply because he couldn't be bothered. He was in a deep depression, suffering the loss of his wife, so he allowed everything to fall apart.

There I was again, pondering Allinson's motives, making excuses for him, *thinking* about him as I did far too much of my time.

"Do you work alone in the stable? No boy to help muck out the stalls or groom the horses?" I turned my questioning to Drover.

"Nope. There be only a few animals to care for. I manage all right. The man before me left suddenly. I hired in temporary and ended up staying." He paused a moment as if exhausted from saying so much.

"Quiet, just me an' the horses. Suits me."

"I imagine." I settled back on the swaying bench for the rest of the ride to town.

Quiet was fine for some—for pretty much everyone who lived at Allinson Hall, apparently. But I was used to a little noise. When I entered the local pub, I inhaled the stench of sweat and sour ale, and blissfully absorbed the chatter and laughter of men enjoying a few hours off work. Although it was only midmorning, big burly farming types took up several of the tables, lifting their glasses and spinning their tales. Even though their northern dialect was as thick as the wool on the sheep most of them raised, this felt like coming home.

Nearly every head in the place turned toward me. Strangers must be rare beasts in these parts. I lifted my hand in greeting and dove into the silence. "Hello. I'm Graham Cowrie, tutor to the Allinson twins."

Blank stares. I didn't think I could stand any more silent walls between me and my fellow human beings. "A round for the house on me," I called to the barkeep.

Immediate smiles and cheers erupted. More than one way to win new friends, I thought, as a man at the nearest table motioned me to an empty chair.

After filling in the blanks about who I supposedly was, answering the country folks' questions about life in the big city, and drinking a pint of stout so thick it could stand alone without a glass, I finally began to nibble away at my new friends' store of knowledge.

In an attempt to be accepted into their circle, I'd modified my accent from "gentleman fallen on hard times" to "lower-class just like you" minus the East End slang I'd grown up using.

"Strange lot up at the big house," I began. "Been there nigh on three weeks, and I still feel like a bad cold everyone wishes would go away."

A murmur of ayes and some chuckles greeted my comment.

George Trent, a farmer who'd delivered a load of hay to the livery stable and was delaying returning home to a mountain of chores, clicked his tongue against his overly large teeth. "Surprised you lasted this long." He bent over the table and lowered his voice. "You *see* anything up there?"

I straightened, my haziness from the overly strong ale evaporating at his words. "See what?"

"You know. *Anything?*" he repeated.

Simple as that, key to a lock, I'd opened a secret cupboard, and gossip spilled out.

"My gal Betty used to be a maid there. Came home after a week, sayin' she'd do millwork rather than go back," a towheaded man named Mortimer shared. "At first I thought maybe Allinson had tried it on with her or summat, but she said it weren't nothin' like that. Said she felt scared all the time, like something 'as watchin' her. Stalkin' her like."

"Aye. My Brian said the same," chimed in another man whose name I couldn't remember. "He were a footman for near a year. Polishing the silver one day when he said a coldness come over him. Seemed all the light was sucked from the room, and he sat in darkness, only the darkness were *inside* him. He could hardly breathe. Leaped up from the table and left the silver where it lay. He never went back."

I blinked. This was much more dramatic than what I'd expected to hear. Of course, stories had a way of being embellished. This certainly went a long way toward explaining the short staff. No one from the village wanted to work at the Hall after hearing such rumors.

"I can't say I've experienced anything quite like that," I said. "From what I've seen, it's nothin' more than an old house with lots of shadows and creaky wood floors. I wonder, do any of you know anything about Mrs. Allinson's death?"

Glances shot back and forth across the table before George finally spoke. "They *say* she died of a sudden fever. That's what was told us. Gone the same night she fell ill."

"But you doubt that?"

Big shoulders shrugged. "All I know's my first wife, Bess, God rest her soul, had pneumonia, and it went on for days before she passed. I never heard of a fever could take someone just that quick."

"No one but the Allinson family at the funeral, Sir Richard and the boys, the vicar said. No chance for local folks to pay respect to the lady, and no out-of-town guests arriving." Mortimer shook his shaggy blond head. "'Twas very odd."

"Aye. Indeed. 'Twas." The others supported him.

I took a sip of the second glass of ale someone had set before me. "What was Lavinia Allinson like?"

"A kind lady. Did her part visiting the sick and organizing the May festival and such." Mortimer paused. "Or she did when she first came here. No one saw her much toward the end, even at the church. Mayhap she was already sick with whatever took her."

"Sick indeed," George scoffed.

"What do *you* think happened to her?" I asked outright.

"I couldn't say. That lot up at the house is closemouthed, shut tight like a widow's pocketbook, but those who've worked up there for a time and aren't so high and mighty about telling tales—"

"Like my Betty," Mortimer added.

"Like Betty," George agreed, "said Mrs. Allinson seemed a real unhappy lady, weeping as she walked in the garden, pale as the belly of a garden slug. Wouldn't come out of her room some days, or she'd go up in the tallest tower and stand looking out the window for hours."

The man whose name I'd forgotten nearly bounced on his chair with excitement. "Our Brian said the same. The day he left, he looked back and saw the missus peering out the tower window. Or *something* was peering," he added in a ghoulish whisper.

The barkeep, a stocky man in an apron, had drifted over to join in on the conversation and fill the glasses. "Ghost stories and rubbish! As the young man says, it's just an old house with creaking floors and falling bits of masonry. Poor Mrs. Allinson was a woman suffering the moodiness all women are prone to from time to time. She was used to the city and likely had a hard time living a quiet country life."

"So she died of sadness?" George scoffed.

"She died of a fever, as we've been told, and you lot are too eager to make up stories to entertain yourselves." The barkeep headed back to his domain behind the bar.

A few more secondhand tales about the Allinsons and the house were shared before the topic shifted to the fall harvest. It seemed I'd gathered all the facts I could from these men and had only learned it was difficult to separate fact from wild rumors. But no one had accused Sir Richard of being a dastardly murderer in any of their stories, whatever they conjectured about Mrs. Allinson's death. Nor did I truly suspect any such thing, or I wouldn't have stayed in the house a moment longer.

I bid my new mates good-bye and was rewarded with a chorus of farewells following me out the door. Whoever said country folk were standoffish with outsiders hadn't met this lot.

The tiny town didn't have much to boast of, but I poked around each shop and examined everything. It felt so good to be someplace other than the Allinson estate. Comparing prices of two almost identical pairs of black gloves in the mercantile store seemed as exciting as shopping in Piccadilly on a crowded Saturday afternoon.

I found the men at the pub weren't the only locals eager to talk to the Allinsons' new tutor and glean whatever gossip they could about the house and its inhabitants.

The baker's wife, after selling me a fresh hot bun, rested her thick arms against the counter and leaned in for a chat. "I ain't the superstitious type m'self, but many say the Hall is haunted. There've been tales about the place since my granny was a lass, strange sights and odd occurrences as was told about by those who worked there. And the Allinson family from generations back was always a bit different, a dour and gloomy lot." She brushed a smudge of flour off her round cheek while I bit into the sweet bun.

"But folks worked there despite the ghosts. A job is a job. Until recently."

"What happened recently?" I prompted.

"Not for me to say, but the way the young Mrs. Allinson passed so sudden seemed not quite right somehow. Not like I believe anyone did her in, as some around these parts have suggested," she scoffed. "Nothing so outlandish. But it's my thought that maybe she…"

The bell rang over the door, and another customer entered.

The baker's wife rocked back on her heels and planted her hands on her hips. "Anything else I can help you with, sir?"

Maybe what? Damn! Now she'd developed scruples about gossiping because someone else was listening in? Damn, damn, damn!

I lingered, hoping to have the baker's wife to myself again, but one customer then another came in, all of them eager to meet the stranger in their midst. I finally had to concede my chance with her was over.

I spent as long as I could in the village, returning to the tavern for a last glass of ale before reluctantly trudging toward home in the late afternoon. I'd told Drover not to wait for me after completing his errands, so I had several miles to walk. Not that I minded, but I suddenly realized I wouldn't make it to the Hall before dark.

Maybe she what? What did the baker's wife suspect? If it wasn't murder, I could only think of one or two other circumstances that would require secrecy. Perhaps Mrs. Allinson had an unwanted pregnancy and tried to terminate it herself with lethal results. But more likely, given what I'd learned about her sad moods, she'd done herself in. Suicide was a stain on a family's name equaled only by insanity—or a sodomite in the family tree. Hiding such things was common.

That extra layer of misery added to the loss of a beloved mother and wife certainly explained the strain between the boys and their father. Likely the lads wouldn't have been told the truth, but they were smart enough to realize something was amiss, and what child doesn't like to lay the blame for all sadness at their parents' door.

The last rosy glow colored the western sky and silhouetted the Hall like a doll's castle on the horizon. I would walk the rest of the way in darkness under growing clouds, but this wild land at night couldn't be more eerie than my destination.

The clear day ended as rain moved in, faster than I'd expected. The first fat drops hit my cheeks, and I sped up my plodding pace. Before I'd trotted another quarter mile, the heavens unleashed. I drew my coat collar as high as I could and pulled my hat down hard over my ears. I had a stitch in my side, and my skin grew icy cold. Teeth chattering, I hurried onward toward the creepy house that now seemed like a cozy haven.

Pounding hoofbeats behind me made me spin around, half expecting a headless horseman to bear down on me as in Irving's tale. The rider approaching was almost as chilling—or perhaps I meant thrilling.

Sir Richard thundered along on his great black steed, heading right at me. I fought an urge to flee like a fox being chased and stood at the side of the road like a drowned rat waiting to board the nearest passing ship.

CHAPTER 10

Allinson drew his mount to a halt so abrutply it reared on its hind legs. I stumbled back from the lethal hooves slashing the air.

The master brought his horse under control with a soft command and a hard pull on the reins. "Whoa. Easy now." His tone was considerably less kind as he turned his attention to me. "Cowrie, what the devil are you doing walking in the rain?"

I looked up, *way* up, at the man towering above me. "It was my day off. I'm just now getting back from the village."

I could barely make out his fearsome scowl in the gathering darkness as he scolded me. "You shouldn't have started so late in the day. And you should've taken a look at the sky first. In this country, you must learn to judge approaching weather."

I tipped my head back even farther so rain bathed my face. "Yes, I rather see that now," I replied dryly.

The horse took a few sideways steps, eager to be moving, smart enough to know a warm stall and oats awaited it. Allinson looked in the direction of the house, at least another half mile away, then at me.

"I'd send the carriage for you, but..." He shook his head in impatience and extended a hand toward me. "Come. I'll give you a ride back."

I blinked away raindrops and gazed at his glove for all of two seconds before eagerly seizing hold. His strong grip held me fast as he pulled me up behind him. I slung an awkward leg over the horse's back with too much zest and nearly slipped off the other side, forcing me to grab a fistful of Allinson's coat to stop my fall. I wrapped my arms around his body as the horse began to move.

Christ, I was going to fall to my death. I was barely seated, and already Sir Richard urged his mount into a canter. I'd mostly walked or occasionally taken cabs to get around the city and could count on one finger the number of times I'd actually ridden a horse. My teeth clicked together as I bounced against that broad muscular back—and I don't mean the horse.

Necessity rather than lust made me cling to Allinson with all my strength, my legs pressed against his, the heat of his body taking the edge off my chill. I wished the saddle weren't in the way so we might be even closer, near enough that my rising erection might rub against his backside. But even with space between us, I felt the flex and flow of muscles in his legs and sides, and I admired how his shoulders stretched the smooth broadcloth coat. He wore no hat, perhaps unable to keep it on given the speed with which he rode—I know my bowler was barely staying on—so his dark hair slicked like sealskin to his head. I longed to cup the curve of his scalp in my palm and feel the heat beneath cool, wet hair.

Heat, indeed. My body was suffused with it from the nearness of the man in my arms. I thought steam might rise off my chilled skin. Such little games we play in our minds. By the time we'd reached the stable yard, I'd already imagined an entire scenario in which we stripped off our soaked clothing and crashed together naked in front of a roaring fire—on a tiger rug, naturally. But my heated fantasy came to an abrupt end when Allinson drew his horse to a halt and I had no more excuse to cling to him.

I reluctantly loosened my arms. Sir Richard dismounted with the grace of a cavalry officer, though he'd never been one, while I half slid, half tumbled off with all the grace of a sack of meal. Allinson grasped his horse's bridle and headed toward the stable.

I stood for a moment, deciding whether to follow him or run for the house. Rain trickled down my neck, and a roll of thunder and flash of lightning got me moving. *In for a penny*, I decided. Determined to spend every second I could in the man's company, I splashed across the yard after Allinson into the dimly lit stable.

"It's all right, Drover. I'll put up Jackdaw myself. You may return to whatever you were doing." Allinson was already removing the horse's saddle as he addressed the groom, who'd emerged from his rooms in the rear of the building.

"Are you certain, sir? I don't mind. It's my job."

But Drover seemed happy enough to concede the point when Sir Richard assured him with a "Yes. Go on now."

He set the saddle aside and removed his dripping greatcoat, laying it over the door of one of the empty stalls before returning to caring for the horse.

I approached from the shadows near the doorway. "Thank you for giving me a ride. I'd be walking still and the rain's coming down harder than ever." In fact, it rattled on the roof like a million tapping fingers.

Allinson glanced at me. "You may go to the house."

"I'd like to help. It's the least I can do to repay you for your kindness." I shed my coat, snatched up a bit of rough toweling as he had done, and hurried to help dry the horse. I looked at the master across the horse's back and offered a smile. "Jackdaw? That's an unusual name."

"Yes." He turned his attention to his task but didn't send me away, so I stayed.

A paraffin lantern lit the interior of the horse barn, which had been built to shelter a dozen mounts. Now only a few of the stalls were occupied. I recognized the bay which had pulled the carriage that brought me here and the wagon I'd hitched a ride on today. A chestnut with a white blaze gazed at us with soulful eyes from the neighboring stall. When we'd finished grooming Jackdaw, he would occupy another. I nearly made a comment about how few horses lived in the large stable, but realized it would seem rude. Sir Richard had a right to keep as many or as few horses as he wished. If he wasn't hosting fox hunts and such, what was the point of having the upkeep of a dozen horses?

The silence in the barn was disturbed only by the rain on the roof, the soft blowing noises the horses made, and their restless movements. It was so quiet, the rasp of sacking against Jackdaw's steaming side sounded too loud, as did my own breathing. I was never one to be comfortable in silence. After a few moments, I had to say something to fill it.

"Did you have a good ride today?"

"Yes," Allinson grunted. He dropped the drying towel and started in with a currycomb.

"That's nice. Where were you off to?" The moment I blurted the question, I knew it was too personal. We weren't mates chatting over ale. One didn't ask one's employer about his business.

But surprisingly, Sir Richard answered. "Checking on one of my tenants."

"Ah," I replied.

"Albert McGrew," he continued. "His family has been farming our land as long as there've been Allinsons in the Hall. But the old man is the last of his line. He had only sisters, who married and moved away, and Albert never took a wife. Recently, neighbors noticed he's neglected his animals and fields, and when they checked on him, the man's speech seemed slurred and irrational."

"Age is cruel." I thought of Clara Weevil, a batty old prostitute I knew who still tried to ply her trade in the pub I frequented. Nothing much sadder to witness than that. I'd bought her a meal now and then, and when I found her passed out drunk on the street, I'd drag her back to the tenement where she squatted.

Allinson's low voice flowed through the air and surrounded me like a warm, rough blanket. "At any rate, something must be done. Albert can't pay rent any longer nor stay in his cottage unattended. No one seems willing to take the man into their home. I suppose one can't blame them. Difficult enough to care for one's own family."

"So what are you going to do?" It was apparent Sir Richard needed a pair of listening ears, which I could supply.

I'd crouched to dry the horse's undercarriage, and now I knelt in the straw to wipe down its tall legs, hocks, and withers or what have you. The scent of wet horse and dry straw nearly made me sneeze.

"I'm not sure yet." He moved around the horse's head and rubbed between its ears. "The last time I had such a quandary, I brought Tom Smith to work in the house, but I don't know if I can find work for Albert to do."

"Maybe he could help Drover in the stables, and the groom could keep an eye on him. He might even appreciate the companionship."

Sir Richard remained quiet a moment, and I feared I'd gone too far, offering my opinion. Then he spoke. "That's not a bad idea. I shall consider it."

I beamed as if he'd petted me on the head, and his response made me bold enough to ask more questions. "What is poor Tom's story?"

Allinson was focused on Jackdaw, so I could study his handsome craggy features illuminated in the lantern's glow. His nose was a sharp blade, and his cheekbones and jaw might cut a caressing hand. Glittering eyes hid in the dark shadows beneath his jutting brow. His mouth was thinned to a line at the moment, but when he relaxed, I'd noticed his lips were full and curved—the only softness to be found in that angular face.

"Tom's family was not kind. They treated him like one of their farm animals, had him sleeping with them for that matter. But one doesn't interfere with families."

"No." I understood all too well. After my father died and Mum took up with the horrible Roger Dwyer, when things got loud and violent, no neighbor tried to help us. It wasn't their place.

"Honestly, it was a blessing when Tom's father drove him off to fend for himself. I was finally able to lend the boy a hand, give him a job and a place to live."

"That was very kind of you."

He shrugged off my praise. "It was my responsibility."

"The boy is smarter than people think," I said. "And he's an incredibly gifted artist. You truly saved him."

"An artist? How would you know that?"

"The first day he came to fetch the lunch trays, the boys were drawing. He seemed so intrigued that I allowed him to join in. Since then, I've been giving him lessons in the evening—in our spare time. I'm not taking him away from his work," I explained. "I hope that's all right."

Allinson had moved around to my side of the horse to brush Jackdaw's neck. He gazed down at me. "He draws well?"

"Astonishingly well. Lithograph quality. Certainly better than anything I could do."

Any more words dried up in my mouth as I gazed at Allinson standing right in front of me. Our positions couldn't have been more suggestive. I was still on my knees, eye level with his groin. *Good evening!* I greeted the bulge in snug riding breeches.

I tore my gaze away from his crotch, praying he hadn't noticed my bald stare, and looked up to his face. He *had* noticed. No doubt about that. Allinson's face flushed, and his jaw worked, clenching and unclenching rhythmically. He was either about to strike me across the face for my impertinence or, God, with any luck, grab my arm, pull me to my feet, and kiss me until neither of us could see straight.

I saw it in my mind almost as if it had already happened. I swore I could feel his crushing arms around my body and the desperation in his kisses. As devoted as Allinson seemed to be to his dead wife, I surmised he had never followed through on his inclination toward men. He seemed the type who'd deny those perverse needs to the bitter end of his days. I envisioned a scenario in which I was the first man to tap those hidden desires, to show him what could be, and to tutor him in the ways of male loving. Between one breath and another, I'd already played out the entire scene in my head.

Our gazes remained entwined in a silent wrestling match. Who would give in first and look away? Who would give in and reach out for what he wanted?

Allinson's shoulders rose and fell with his breathing. He gripped that currycomb as if it were a life preserver. His lips parted slightly and I held my breath, waiting.

"No." That was all he muttered. Just the one word.

It was a dagger of disappointment to my heart. But lust still swirled in the air between us, so powerful and palpable, it felt almost like another presence in the room. I rose slowly to my feet and cocked my head slightly. "No?"

Confusion knit his dark brows over eyes that gleamed with desire.

Oh *yes*, he wanted me, and I knew how to make him want me even more. I could easily steer this situation to its natural conclusion. A heated look, a teasing smile, my hands unfastening those tight breeches, and then back on my knees and…

I could also find myself out of a job come morning. Hell, I probably would anyway. Having gone this far, why not push further? I took another step closer to Allinson. So close I could smell his delicious sweat, hear the creak of his leather boots as he shifted, practically taste his salty skin when I inhaled.

Allinson swayed a fraction, his body inclining toward mine as if drawn by a magnet. Then he pulled back.

"No! Not here. Not now." He seemed to realize his mistake. "Or *ever*," he gritted between his teeth, his shocked eyes going narrow.

As he turned away, I heard another whisper meant only for himself. "Not again."

My ears pricked. *Again?* So he wasn't completely inexperienced as I'd assumed. There was a story there, a loss of something precious, another thread in a tapestry of tragedy. Another question to add to my long list.

I had darted my fingers through flames for long enough. Time to draw back before I got a serious burn. Allinson had made his feelings clear. Even if he was interested, he wasn't interested. I should respect that and stop playing the coquette.

I resumed drying the already dry horse. "So, Jackdaw. How did you come to choose that name?"

Allinson threw me a look over his shoulder as he strode toward the oat bin. "I should think that would be fairly obvious."

"Yes, of course. He's black and glossy like a crow. I guess Crow or Raven would be an odd name. Jackdaw sounds better." I began to babble, the confidence I displayed in flirtatious situations abruptly dispersing.

"There was an old peg-legged sailor used to live in my building. He kept a raven in a cage. Seemed cruel to me. I snuck into his place and let it out one day."

Recalling that I was meant to be a genteel man who'd only recently been forced to assume teaching positions, I snapped my mouth closed on any more stories of the colorful inhabitants of the shabby tenement where I'd most recently lived. My accent was slipping too. I righted it like a woman adjusting her hat and jabbing in a couple of pins.

Sir Richard poured oats into Jackdaw's feedbox, and the horse moved away from me to docilely enter his stall. His master stroked the beast's neck and didn't turn toward me again as he said, "Thank you for your help. You may go now."

"Yes. All right. And thank *you* again for saving me from a long, wet walk."

I had no more excuse for lingering. I put on my coat and headed out into the rain, jogging swiftly toward the house.

I mentally ran through the events of the last hour, with some imagined embellishments, and realized that something had shifted. In telling his worries about old Albert McGrew, Sir Richard had opened a door through which confidences might be exchanged.

And in that magnetic moment when we'd been a breath away from giving in to temptation, that door had been taken off its proverbial hinges. I couldn't help but believe that sooner or later, one or the other of us would walk through it.

CHAPTER 11

Over the next week, the weather announced that winter truly was just around the corner. Every day was overcast, blustery, and sometimes rainy. The boys and I couldn't spend more than five minutes outdoors before freezing wind drove us back inside. With that loss of freedom and sunlight, a gloom settled over me again.

This despair was much deeper and longer lasting than the previous brief bouts I'd experienced since coming to Allinson Hall. In my life, I'd known hard times and had lost loved ones, but I'd never experienced such a debilitating hopelessness. It took every ounce of my strength to drag my body out of bed and adopt a cheery demeanor for the twins' benefit. My responsibility to those boys was the beacon that kept me from wallowing in darkness. I was there for them, and to me that meant much more than their education. I'd grown quite fond of the lads and protective of their wellbeing and happiness.

Everyone in the household either accepted or ignored the fact Clive never spoke. At first, I'd been too new to bring up the subject, particularly with the master of the house. But as I grew more confident in my position as the boys' teacher and caretaker, I decided it was time to address the issue.

I resolved to seek out Sir Richard and discuss both of his sons' welfare, whether or not he wanted to hear what I had to say. But first I would try to learn just a little more about the center of this storm of intense emotions, Lavinia Allinson. Such a sensitive topic must be broached carefully with the twins.

An opportunity presented itself one day during our afternoon art time as I looked over Clive's shoulder at his drawing—yet another depiction of a woman haloed in light facing a sinister entity. Whitney had gone to use the WC, and Clive and I were alone in the schoolroom.

"Who is the woman, Clive? Your mum?"

He ignored me and scrubbed with the side of his pencil to make the dark being even blacker. But then he inclined his head slightly.

I squatted so I was on his level. "And this?" I pointed to the darkness. "What is this thing?"

Of course he didn't answer, so I elaborated. "Something bad happened?"

His hand stopped moving.

I lowered my voice. "I understand. My father, brother, and two of my sisters died almost all at once. Death felt like a monster that snatched them away. But it's all right to talk about it. You might feel better if you did."

He viciously blackened the figure still further.

I tried again. "Death is not—"

He crumpled up the paper and threw it across the room.

"Clive…" I touched his shoulder, to try to offer some small comfort, but the boy bolted out of his chair, knocking it into me so I lost my balance and nearly fell over.

By the time I scrambled to my feet, he'd left the room. I was frustrated and disappointed. He seemed to tolerate my presence better these days, and I'd hoped to reach him, but it seemed we were back to square one. Maybe I'd get a better response from Whit.

Except neither boy returned. I waited nearly twenty minutes before admitting they'd done a runner on me. If they hadn't braved the bad weather to hide out in their secret garden, then they were lurking in any of the hundred and some rooms in this ridiculous place. I was reminded how little control I actually had over my charges. I might have won their interest and trust for a short while, but keeping it was another thing.

With nothing better to occupy my time and feeling that I ought to at least *attempt* to keep track of the boys, I set out to hunt for them. I guessed they'd head for the older part of the building, so I walked the now-familiar path into the fortress that was the heart of Allinson Hall. A chill rose from the unforgiving stone to envelope me.

I carried a small lamp in my hand, which did little to dispel the somber gloom that filled not only the corridor but my spirit as well. Every step took me farther from the present and into the past. I explored bedchambers and the chapel, where I half hoped I might encounter Sir Richard again. But the darkness there was undisturbed, no candles burned, nor did any presence flit at the corner of my vision.

I moved on, not really expecting to find Whit and Clive, who knew how to keep out of sight and might be spying on me as I searched. Like cats, they'd show up when they wished.

I turned a corner, and there it was—the door to the tower. Slightly ajar once more. My stomach thudded into my shoes as I stared at the slice of darkness and recalled the sensation of something—not a lock—holding the door shut against me. I told myself to go back. I had nothing to prove here. No one would consider me braver because I'd gone up those stairs. And if something should happen, if I should trip and fall all the way down, I might break my neck, and it could be days, if ever, before anyone found me.

However, the boys might be playing up there. If they were, there was no way for them to get past me. I'd have them cornered and coerce them into returning to the schoolroom where they belonged.

If they weren't there? Curiosity went a long way toward getting my feet moving again. I *had* to see. I had to know what the room or rooms at the top of the tower looked like. I had to see the view for myself.

"You've faced down bullies and been in pub brawls. This is not a real danger. It's just a dark, cobwebbed, ancient, eerie, creepy, possibly haunted place. Now go!" I ordered myself aloud.

I reached out a shaking hand to grasp the handle and pull the door the rest of the way open. I shone my lamp into the narrow passage to reveal nothing but the stairs. Then I set my foot on the first step.

Any time in my life I've had to face fear, I've done it by counting. I would tell myself, *In a mere X amount of minutes, this will be over, so why indulge in being upset? Get through the next several seconds, and this will become a part of the past, an artifact to be remembered but with no power over me.* The method worked quite well when Dwyer was beating the snot out of me.

One step, two steps, three steps, four. No cold air—at least not any colder than the rest of the fortress—and no whispering voices disturbed the stillness. Nor did I hear the giggles or pattering feet of children from overhead. Whit and Clive probably weren't up there.

I peered ahead into the well of darkness that seemed to absorb my little light. I couldn't see a damned thing beyond the few steps in front of me. How many stairs were there to the top of the tower—and what awaited me there?

Twelve, thirteen, fourteen. I could go back down any time. Just turn around and trot down those stairs—not run because nothing was after me, but—*eighteen, nineteen, twenty*—I was almost at the top. What was the point in going this far and giving up? A quick peek around a probably empty guard tower, one look at the view of the land below, and my curiosity would be satisfied once and for all.

The backs of my legs ached, and I was out of breath from the climb as much as my own superstitious nerves when I reached the top landing. Another door confronted me. Closed this time. Did I have the nerve to creak it open on what would surely be a pair of rusty hinges? Every skeletal specter from the many ghastly stories I'd read haunted my mind as I reached for the handle. Nothing would expel them quicker than facing whatever lay on the other side.

I took hold of the metal grip, turned, and pushed. The door swung inward as silently as a casket lid to reveal more darkness. I held up my lamp and stepped inside.

See? Nothing to fear here. It's just an empty room. The ceiling vaulted into a peak, an intersecting framework of beams supporting the conical roof. No wreaths of cobwebs occupied by fat spiders were spun here. No rats, mice, or even pigeons or roosting bats.

A single straight-backed wooden chair stood near one of several windows cut through the thick stone walls. These five narrow windows hardly allowed any light to enter the chamber. I frowned and looked from one window to the next, all the way around the circular room. Literally almost *no* light, which was very odd. Certainly the day was cloudy but there should have been some weak beams illuminating the room. Yet, though I could see the light outside, none seemed to pierce the interior darkness. The hair on my neck prickled with unease at the unnatural phenomenon.

I'd come too far to simply flee back down the stairs. I'd have one good look around the room, then never come here again. I padded over the stone floor, skirting an irregular dark stain in the center of the floor, and stopped by the chair near the south window. This was the same window I'd seen a light shining from on my first night here.

Which begged another question. With five windows, why had light shone only from this one? And who would have been up here to light a lantern?

I rested my hand on the chair back, feeling smooth wood as I gazed around the barren space. That dark stain on the floor. Was it lamp oil? Blood? What had spilled, and had it happened generations ago or more recently? I tore my mind away from wild imaginings and went to look out the window. A card of some kind rested on the sill. I touched a fingertip to it and left an imprint in the dust.

As I picked it up and blew off the dust, a feeling of pure desolation rolled through me in a wave. My entire body tensed, trying to fight it off. Tears spilled down my cheeks, and I caught back a sob. What the *hell* was happening to me? Emotions not my own invaded me. I seized hold of myself, recalling who I was—a man who could make light of anything, a man who never gave in to adversity and joked in the face of troubles. I was not a creature of sorrow but of, if not joy, then at least an affable disposition. This sadness did not suit me.

I wiped away the barrage of sudden tears and opened the folder. Inside were two photographs facing each other. Nearly mirror images, but I knew immediately the babies were Clive and Whitney. Amazing that the children had held still long enough for clear photographs to be taken.

My boys. Another powerful emotion filled me with an instinctual possessiveness at the sight of their chubby, somber little faces. I would protect them. I would stand between them and anything that threatened them. It was more than a duty. My heart demanded it.

The feeling subsided, leaving me empty and shaken and utterly perplexed. True, I'd grown quite fond of Whitney and Clive but they weren't mine to love in such an intense way. Besides, what evil threatened them? Not their father. I no longer believed he'd harmed them or ever would. Nor had he done away with his wife. So, what in the world was I meant to protect them *from*?

I shook off the residue of that blaze of emotion and placed the folder with the boys' photographs on the vacant chair, where I was quite certain Lavinia had sat for hours on end, thinking her morose thoughts. Whatever had happened in this room, I no longer wanted to know about it.

I turned to leave, and my blood froze to ice in my veins. The door was closed. Less than a minute before, I'd entered the room, leaving it wide open. I'd never heard it shut. I *knew* I would find it locked—or held closed in a more mysterious way. I was trapped in the tower room. No one knew where I was. I would die like one of Poe's hapless victims, the man in "The Cask of Amontillado" or the wife in "The Black Cat," both sealed into walls to slowly starve to death or suffocate. No one would hear me screaming for help.

Beyond the edge of my sight, something with no discernable shape moved. I couldn't begin to describe it, and perhaps it was more of a *feeling* than a movement. Something pitch-black and formless, something that filled me with dread. Icy coldness seeped into my very bones, making my body tremble and my teeth chatter. The cloying stench of decay filled the room. And I knew beyond a shadow of doubt that an entity devoid of any emotion other than destruction wanted something from me.

My heart thundered, and my blood unfroze to rush through my ears. I hurtled myself at the door to grasp the handle and haul on it with all my strength. When the heavy door immediately and easily swung open, I stumbled backward. Nearly sobbing with relief, I plunged down the spiral staircase, taking steps two and three at a time. Would I reach the bottom only to find *that* door closed?

But it remained ajar as I'd left it. I raced through, not bothering to close it behind me, and pounded down the hallway as if the hounds of hell chased me.

CHAPTER 12

Not until I was back in what I'd come to consider the safe part of the house did I slow down and draw breath. Foolish, fanciful man to believe "ghosties and ghoulies and long-legged beasties and things that go bump in the night" existed. I truly was a victim of my own overactive imagination. I'd given myself heart palpitations over an empty room and a couple of doors that reacted to sagging hinges, gravity, and warped frames.

My logical mind had to explain it all away, because the alternative—that something or several things lurked in the tower, or perhaps in this entire cursed place—was untenable. Those powerful, almost maternal emotions I'd felt had to be a strange figment of my mind and not the ghost of a dead woman. And that threatening darkness that began to take shape at the periphery of my vision was nothing but a trick of the light.

I splashed the perspiration from my face and changed the shirt I'd sweated through before returning to the schoolroom. If the boys weren't there, I'd tidy up, prepare for future lessons, and maybe work on my would-be novel.

But both Whitney and Clive lay on their stomachs on the floor, playing with tin soldiers like little angels.

"Did you have a good break?" I asked sarcastically before settling cross-legged on the rug between them. "I understand it's no fun being cooped up inside. I feel the same way. We can't do lessons all the time."

Whit glanced up, at least acknowledging my presence. Clive didn't.

I sighed. Forward two steps and back four. I wasn't gaining any headway with Clive, and my mentioning his mother today had only made things worse.

Take them to their father. The simple, clear message dropped into my mind without my summoning it. *What?* I asked. But the directive only grew stronger, more implacable. *Take them now.*

I gazed from one towhead to the other and at the twins' busy hands moving their troops into position for battle. Sir Richard had given me one directive—keep the boys occupied and learning. He'd never once suggested he wanted to see them or even be informed of their progress. In fact, it was almost as if he'd like to forget they existed. His negligence frustrated me and flared hotly now. I'd take them to him, all right. Force him to acknowledge their presence.

I scrambled to my feet. "Boys, what say we go on an expedition? Like Stanley in Africa, we'll see what we can discover."

Both boys looked up at me. I'd hooked their interest that much.

"It's raining outside," Whit pointed out.

"It is. But the expedition I propose is a literary one. Has either of you ever read *Robinson Crusoe*?"

Two blond heads shook in unison.

"Then your lives have been sorely lacking. It's the most thrilling adventure tale ever, about a man shipwrecked on an island, struggling to survive and facing incredible dangers. I propose we go in hunt of this book in the library. It must be there somewhere."

Clive clicked his tongue, and the flicker of excitement in both pairs of eyes dimmed. "That's not a real expedition," Whitney scoffed.

"It is if we make it one." I tapped my temple. "Use your imagination. Come on."

They were still young enough to be fooled by a little bit of theater. We all suited up as if going on a real expedition, using whatever props we found among the boys' toys. Coiled rope, wooden guns, a lantern—which we actually needed in the dimly lit corridors—and a packet of biscuits for provisions to eat along the journey.

We started out, taking many side trips along the way, past a carpet of quicksand we must navigate around, a sofa crocodile that lurked in the parlor, and a mirror of doom which would turn one to stone if he looked into it.

Whit abandoned his worldly-wise attitude and joined in my inventing. "Shh, I hear natives coming!" We hunkered down, flat against the wall, and waited for the footsteps to pass.

The maid, Molly, came around the corner and shrieked at the unexpected sight of us squatting on the floor. She dropped the stack of sheets she was carrying.

I put my hands up. "Have no fear, native woman. We will not harm you. We are but explorers in this strange land. We come in peace."

The boys and I quickly gathered her laundry and delivered it back into her arms. Molly gazed at us as if we were quite mad before hurrying on her way.

At last we reached our destination and opened the library door. Would we find the tiger in his book-jungle lair? Or must I hunt him down in another part of the house, perhaps his study or the billiard room? Because the insane command continued to hammer in my brain. *Take them to him.*

I didn't immediately see Allinson in his chair near the fire, but there were enough bookcases and alcoves where he might be hidden. This truly would be a hunt. On my last trip to the library, I'd noted there seemed to be no rhyme or reason to the way books were shelved. Finding *Robinson Crusoe*—if the book was even there—would be a hunt in itself.

"All right, lads, we've reached the heart of the Congo." I took off my pack with the provisions and set it on the floor. "Time to fan out and begin our search."

I offered them each a piece of paper. "This is how the title is spelled. The path to the prize may be long and arduous. You may have to read many book covers in order to find it, and even then, success is not guaranteed. But we are explorers, men. It is our destiny to search these uncharted lands."

Whit was on board now and seized the paper before running off to the nearest bookshelf. Clive gave me a more cynical look and rolled his eyes as he took my note.

"Good luck," I said.

Clive headed toward the far wall, where a bank of books awaited him. Just as he reached it, Allinson emerged from the rear of the room, around a freestanding bookcase, with a volume in his hand.

"What's going on here?" he asked, not angrily but seeming amused by what he'd overheard. A smile curved his lips and made his dark eyes sparkle. I fell a little bit in love at the beautiful sight.

But Clive stared at his father as if he were a demon conjured from thin air, and began to back away. Immediately, Sir Richard's smile disappeared and the habitual air of sorrow settled on him once more.

I'd had quite enough of the whole mysterious mess. I grabbed hold of Clive's shoulder as he started to sidle away, gently but firmly not allowing him to leave. "Good afternoon, sir. I thought I'd bring the boys to the library to find a few volumes they might enjoy. Have you a copy of *Robinson Crusoe*, by any chance?"

I felt the tension in Clive's thin shoulder and gave him a gentle squeeze of encouragement. *Stick by me, boy, and together we'll face the tiger.* Whatever frightened him so about his father, it was time to confront it. Meanwhile, I noticed Whit had crept as far as the door, but he wouldn't leave a man behind, so he stayed there.

"Yes, I'm certain there's a copy, and probably more than one. Let me look." Sir Richard turned away to study one of the shelves.

I leaned to whisper to Clive. "Why don't you help him look?" I gave the boy a push toward his father, then beckoned to Whit. "You go and help too."

There! Have I done what you wanted? I've taken them to their father.

Feeling smug and satisfied, I watched my handiwork. The two little boys approached Sir Richard like game hunters sneaking up on quarry, respectful of the wild animal in their midst. Clive stopped at the farthest end of the shelf as he could possibly get and pretended to look at the books. But he kept a watchful eye on the tall man.

"Ah, here it is." Allinson pulled a brown-covered book from the shelf and read aloud, The Life and Strange Surprising Adventures of Robinson Crusoe of York, Mariner. He flipped idly through the pages. "It's been years since I've read it. I'm sure you boys will find it quite exciting."

He walked toward Clive with the book extended, the smile returning to his face.

Clive, with Whitney just behind him, seemed poised to run away but held his ground. He stared into his father's eyes as he took the book, and for several moments, their gazes remained joined. Then Clive and Whit backed away slowly, never taking their eyes off their father.

I watched this silent drama play out and felt utterly useless. I didn't know how to help the boys and Allinson repair what was broken, and it wasn't my place to interfere.

"Whitney, thank your father," I said.

"Thank you, sir." The mumble was so soft, I could barely hear from where I stood a short distance away. Whit glanced at me as he passed me. "We'll go back to our room now. We don't need any more books."

The boys slipped from the room, and the door closed behind them. I faced Sir Richard, and all thought of deference or rules about the way one ought to address a superior evaporated.

"What is wrong? Why do they seem to fear you so?" I demanded. "I can't help them reconcile with their mother's death and the problems they have with you if I don't understand what happened."

Sir Richard's face was an impenetrable wall he retreated behind. "Mr. Cowrie, it is none of your concern. You're here to teach a few subjects. That is all."

I'm generally a good-natured fellow, but my temper flared. "You're wrong, sir. My duty requires a great deal more than that. Those boys were directionless and unattended when I arrived. I've done much more for them than teach a little arithmetic and spelling. I've cared for them and tried to relieve some of their unhappiness. Do you realize Clive doesn't speak? Not at all! Or if he does, it's only to his brother."

My irritation was building up steam. Though my employer's expression was thunderous, I kept going. "They're trying to recover from their mother's death, but it seems they've lost their father too. You never display any affection toward them. Those boys need your love, some gesture to show them you care."

I knew the burning heat in my cheeks made my face fiery red. As flushed as I felt was how pale Allinson became. The hollows under his eyes and cheekbones seemed darker than ever. He would snap now and throw me out of his house once and for all.

"I've told you they believe I killed their mother. And I don't blame them. Her death *was* my fault." His admission was a hollow whisper that filled the entire room louder than a shout. "It's my fault she did it."

"What did she do?" I prodded relentlessly. "You can tell me. I would never betray your confidence, I swear."

He rubbed a hand over his forehead, then let it drop heavily to his side in a gesture of surrender. "I couldn't make her happy. In fact, I made her miserable."

My immediate instinct was to comfort. "I'm sure that's not true." I took a step toward him.

Allinson looked at me, not in the distant way an employer views an underling, but as a man regards a confidante. "God knows, I tried to behave properly." He gestured in the direction of the door. "Those two boys are proof of how hard I tried, and for a while, they seemed enough to keep her happy, but I couldn't…"

We both knew what he was talking about. No need to pretend otherwise. "You couldn't love her in the way she wanted to be loved. I've had friends back in the city, good family men who kept up the pretense. Many men must do so."

"The first few years, I believe we both tried to put on a good face and accept the match we'd made, but time wears one down." He trailed a fingertip along the row of book spines, *bump, bump, bump.* "And by the end, her loneliness was too great. She hanged herself."

I caught my breath, surprised he'd confided it so bluntly and afraid of saying something that might make him stop. "Those who are prone to deep inner sorrow may suffer even under good circumstances. I knew a man once, the jolliest fellow one could hope to know. No one could believe it when he leaped into the Thames. You mustn't blame yourself."

"I saw her fading by the day and did nothing to help her. Perhaps living in the city, breaking away from the eternal gloom of this place, might have made some difference in lifting her spirits." He bowed his head as if unable to meet my gaze. "And near the end, she learned the truth about me, saw something she never should have seen. I tell you, her death *was* my fault."

I bit my lip and considered. He was adamant about his guilt. It didn't seem I could alleviate it, so I'd try a different angle. "What about the boys? Why does Clive particularly cast you as a villain?"

Sir Richard gripped the edge of the bookshelf with both hands, bracing himself. "He saw. He was the one who found her hanging there."

I swallowed lead as I imagined the pure horror of such a discovery. "In her room?" But I already knew the answer.

"Up in the old guard tower, where she used to sit and gaze out the windows for hours on end." He gave a harsh bark of laughter. "That alone should've alerted me. Instead, I chose to ignore her odd behavior. If I'd sent her to a sanitarium for treatment, perhaps Lavinia would be alive today."

"But no more with her boys than she is now," I pointed out. "Those places are not pleasant. I knew a man once who was treated for malaise at a sanitarium with cold-water baths and electric-shock therapy. I would not highly recommend it."

He glanced at me. "It seems you've had a number of unusual friends."

"My checkered past. But let us speak of the matter at hand, Clive's seeming inability—or unwillingness—to speak."

"Also my fault." Allinson straightened, and his hands gripped in loose fists by his sides. "After he ran to find me, I had to explain to him he must never tell anyone what he'd seen. You know how society treats families of suicides. I couldn't allow my sons' lives to be ruined by having the information spread."

I wanted to point out that the boys' lives had been fairly ruined by both Lavinia's death and the secrecy afterward. Certainly Whit must know all this too, since the boys shared everything. They were all locked in silent conspiracy together.

"The only others in the house who know the truth of her passing are Tom, who helped me cut down and carry her body away, and Smithers. I couldn't keep the local doctor from seeing the ligature marks on her neck, but he is not the type to break his oath of privacy." Allinson looked at me. "And now you."

"I promise I won't breathe a word, and I'll do everything I'm able to help your sons through their grieving."

His deep-set eyes glistened. "I believe you will. You are a tonic for the soul."

Heat flared in my cheeks again at the compliment. If he only knew how I'd lied to land this post, he wouldn't be so generous. "And anything I can do to help *you*, sir, I will gladly do. You are grieving too."

I took another couple of steps until I stood before Sir Richard. I rested a hand on his arm, intent only on offering solidarity and loyalty. But the attraction between us was too strong for even an innocent gesture to remain so. Allinson looked at me with those lovely, shiny eyes, and my heart missed several beats. Was this it? Would this be the moment we both finally gave in to desire?

I grasped his other arm so I held him loosely, and we continued to remain lost in each other's regard. Did I dare? Yes, I did. I moved another step closer and drew Allinson toward me, unresisting. I wrapped my arms around his stiff body and held on. A shudder passed through him. The tension suddenly fled from him as he leaned into my embrace.

My own eyes prickled at his capitulation, and I hugged tighter. Sir Richard wasn't the only one who needed some comforting. My experiences in the tower room were still fresh in my mind, and the emotional upheaval had taken its toll. We remained that way for several moments, leaning into each other like a pair of drunks straggling home from a pub in the wee hours.

Then I made the mistake of talking.

"It's all right," I crooned as I rubbed a hand up his broad back. "Things will get better. You simply need to forgive yourself and find your way back to your boys."

Sir Richard immediately stiffened, and I made the further mistake of cupping my hand round the nape of his neck and giving a gentle knead.

Now he drew back completely and thrust me away from him.

"Stop! Stop it at once." His expression was anguished, so full of pain and confusion I knew immediately I'd gone too far.

"I'm sorry. I was only trying to offer comfort." I held up my empty hands.

"I know very well what you were offering. I don't want it or need it. Leave now," he thundered, pointing an imperious finger at the door.

Aw, Christ. I'd really put my foot in it. "Do you mean for me to pack my things and, uh…"

His Adam's apple bobbed above his crisp shirt collar. "No. The boys' disposition has improved since you've been here. I wouldn't deprive them of the only person apparently capable of making them laugh and play. No, don't leave. Just get out of my sight—and don't attempt anything like that with me again. Do you understand?"

"Yes, sir."

I fled from the library nearly as quickly as I'd run away from the tower. This house was full of scary things of one sort or another. Not the least of which was the growing emotions inside me for the master of the house. If Sir Richard would allow it, I could become quite close to him, and that would be the ultimate danger to my heart.

CHAPTER 13

Days passed after that confession in the library, and I became Sisyphus pushing a boulder up a hill. Though the boys and I fell back into our routine, I didn't feel I made much progress in getting them to truly talk to me. As for their moody father, he still made no effort to spend any time with the twins.

It was an exercise in frustration. I couldn't *force* this family to repair its broken bonds, even while that voice inside continually nagged at me to *Help them.*

Not to mention a deep melancholy possessed me some days, making it difficult to even get out of bed, let alone move through the day. It was like trying to walk in deep water, a strong current tugging at me while a different inner voice suggested I give in and allow the current to carry me away.

Other days, I was my normal self again, strong, capable, and more liable to see a glass as half-full rather than nearly empty. But I had to fight hard every day to keep the negative emotions at bay and to maintain a cheerful attitude for the boys' sake.

During one of Tom's almost nightly art sessions, he drew a picture that could have illustrated one of the more lurid pulp novels. A woman bound by her wrists, arms stretched above her head and a man doing…something to her. The angle at which Tom had drawn the man with his back to the viewer, his face obscured, and his body concealing exactly what he was doing to the lady still left no doubt the act wasn't pleasurable for her. The woman's body bowed away from him, and a pool of something darkened the floor around her feet.

"What is this?" I demanded, so shocked by the scene that I didn't use my usual soothing tone with Tom.

"Evil man," he mumbled.

I noted a pair of slitted windows in the background. "In the tower?"

He nodded.

"Did this actually happen? When?"

"Long ago."

I realized he'd drawn the man in some sort of tunic and leggings, suggesting a by-gone era.

"Did you make up this story, Tom? Who is the man supposed to be?"

"A killer, Great-Grandda says. Long ago."

This was the most Tom had ever spoken all at once. He might have been spewing vast paragraphs. I died to know more details, but that was all I could draw out of him that night, a suggestion of a crime that might or might not have happened a very long time ago. My continued questioning merely frightened Tom and caused him to scurry off.

It was a beginning, something to prop up the notion I'd developed that there might be two distinct entities haunting the Hall: Lavinia and some evil being. But this new bit of knowledge moved me no closer to figuring out what I could do about any of it.

Meanwhile, I also agonized over an entirely different issue—the throb of lust that filled me whenever I recalled my embrace with Allinson in the library. I relived it far too often. I tried to chalk up my unreasonably strong reaction to being away from the possibility of random lovers for over a month with no hand but my own to give me sexual relief. But deep down, I knew these feelings were something more than a purely physical reaction.

Wounded, tortured Richard Allinson touched me deeply, awakening every nurturing instinct I had and making me long to hold him. Feeling him close by somewhere in this big house made it all the harder to bear the unbridgeable distance between us. I *wanted*, I *needed* with the sort of irresistible force it seemed impossible to deny forever.

One night, after an evening of racing with the boys up and down corridors until we were all tired enough to sleep deeply, I surfaced from a nightmare of drowning.

No, not drowning, but suffocating from something tightening around my neck, I realized as I gasped for air. Drenched in sweat, my heart rate as erratic as a butterfly's wings, I thought I might have actually stopped breathing for a few moments before I woke myself.

I sat up in bed with damp sheets tumbled around me, inhaling and exhaling for the sheer joy of being able to do so. Just as I'd gotten my panic under control, footsteps in the hallway outside my door sent my heart racing again.

I rose up on my knees and listened to the measured tread of someone approaching and stopping in front of my door. I peered into the darkness and waited for the door to open. Good God, why hadn't I locked it? But my next thought was that it didn't make any difference. If some creature wanted to get to me, it would find its way in, locked door or not. I clutched at my bedcovers as if they would protect me and waited.

A moment later, the footsteps moved on. Not a ghost or two small boys, but a grown person lingering outside my bedchamber. I had to see who it was, though it wasn't hard to guess who and why he'd paused by my door. Maybe I wasn't the only one reliving those moments in the library.

I leaped onto the floor, cold even through the rug. Barefoot and wearing only my nightshirt, I padded to the door and hesitated only a second or two before opening it. The corridor was empty.

I lit a lamp and made my way to Whit and Clive's room to check on them—just in case someone more sinister than their father walked the halls. One cot was empty. The boys occupied a single bed, their blond heads sharing a pillow, both of them sound asleep. I thought of the twins in the womb that way, curved around each other, sleeping and waking together in limbo. After being that close for so long, it was a wonder they could ever bear to be apart.

I closed the door softly and started to pad back to my room. I doubted I'd sleep, but I might read until dawn. A flash of something blue farther down the hall caught my attention. By the time I focused, it was gone.

I hurried after it, around the corner. Nothing there. I started to turn back, but once again a movement far ahead in the shadows beckoned me onward. The trailing skirt of a dress? I hurried to catch up.

Down hallways and up stairways, the bit of blue lured me like a bird fluttering just beyond reach. Once more I found myself in front of the chapel door. I pushed the door open.

The chamber was darker than last time I'd visited. A single lit candle graced the altar. Its light glinted off a metal flask that Sir Richard lifted to his mouth. The man sprawled in the front pew, long legs stretched in front of him, no shoes on his stocking feet. Nor did he wear a coat, waistcoat, or tie, only his shirt, unbuttoned at the throat, cuffs loosened. Not only his clothes but his hair was in disarray. The rumpled locks and disheveled clothing made him seem younger, but when he rose and turned toward me, he was a fully grown and intimidating man.

"You followed me?"

I followed something. I didn't bother to explain. "Your footsteps woke me."

He swayed a little, took another swallow from the flask, and beckoned me with it. "Come here."

I could no more have refused his order than the Light Brigade would have refused their commander before that famous charge. I set down my lantern and went to him, smelling the stench of alcohol before I reached him. Not just a little drunk. Falling-down-and-passing-out drunk. And angry drunk, I guessed as I gazed into his eyes.

"Why?" He slurred the one word.

Why was I there? Why were we attracted to each other? Why wouldn't I leave him alone? I didn't know what his question was, but a second later, it didn't matter. He seized hold of me, hauled me up against him, and pressed a single bruising kiss to my mouth before jerking away.

"Don't look at me." He turned me around, and I felt his hardness pushing against my backside. My own cock rose in solidarity—*Yes, friend, I will join you in this endeavor.* I could hardly breathe, I wanted his rough hands all over me so badly. And then they were.

Allinson bent my upper body over the altar and gathered up my nightshirt to bare my legs and arse. His palms stroked from my waist down, gliding over my naked flesh, touching, kneading, sending fireworks through my body. He raked the tip of his thumb up my crack, and my hole clenched in anticipation. My legs shook as I lay sprawled with my cheek against cold granite like some sacrificial virgin. I listened to Richard fumble at his fly and curse when he couldn't get his drunken fingers to cooperate.

I was no stranger to a little rough play. I'd welcomed it on many an occasion, but when Allinson muttered, "God forgive me," I knew this time it was wrong.

I began to straighten. He grasped the back of my neck and forced me down again.

I shook off his grip and lurched upright, turning toward him. "No. I'm up for a bit a fun, but not wit' you hatin' yourself for it. Look at me," I demanded and waited for his bleary eyes to focus on mine. "There's nuffin' evil here. Fuckin's as natural as breathin'. You hafta believe that. No shame or guilt, or I'll have none of it, awright?"

Richard blinked, and I realized I'd gone East Ender in the heat of the moment. I quickly repaired my posh accent. "Do you understand me?"

I pressed my palm against his chest over his rapidly beating heart. "Relax. Let yourself enjoy this. And, for tonight, let me bring you off another way."

He nodded mutely, his eyes glazed and body visibly quivering from excitement. I knew better than to think he'd suddenly mastered his guilt or sobered up, but at that point, I didn't much care. I wanted him too badly to let anything interrupt what came next.

I dragged my hands down from his chest, over his rigid abdomen, to the top of his trousers, which I deftly unfastened. A quick tug over narrow hips, and both trousers and smalls came down. His cock thrust forward, thick and proud, clearly unashamed to declare *its* position on what should happen.

Our bodies are often so much wiser than our brains, I thought as I sank to my knees on hard stone.

For a few seconds, I simply stroked my fist up and down his length, and gazed at Richard's shocked and eager expression. So lovely to see him come undone. I continued to watch his reaction when I brought the flushed tip to my lips and gave it a long, slow, wet kiss. His eyes nearly closed, and breath hissed between his teeth. He swayed. Fearful his legs might buckle and he'd collapse on me, I took hold of the sharp blades of his hips and backed him against the altar so he could brace himself.

Once more I took hold of warm, firm flesh, so satisfyingly heavy in my hand. "Are you ready?" I asked.

He nodded.

"No guilty feelings?"

He shook his head obediently, a compliant drunk now rather than an angry one.

I licked his length, savoring the salt and musk, then drew him deeply into my mouth. Richard groaned. His knuckles whitened as his fingers gripped the edge of the altar. I withdrew his cock and admired the gleaming wet length before sucking again. Richard gave another satisfied groan and wore an expression of utter ecstasy when I glanced at his face.

My own cock ached with the need for a touch, but I promised it that would come later. I continued to focus on giving the best oral gratification I could. I had quite a lot of expertise, and I practiced every trick I knew, light bites and licks, fingernail scratches up the length, ball sucking, thigh nibbling, bunghole probing while simultaneously taking his cock deep into my throat. One thing I was quite good at was making a fellow come.

Once I'd settled into relentless sucking, driving Richard ever upward, I didn't stop until his body began to tense. His upper body angled away from me, half draped over the altar as he leaned back on his elbows. His head rolled back, exposing his throat, and his chest rose and fell rapidly. The sight of this powerful man made vulnerable was so beautiful, I couldn't drag my gaze away as I forced him over the edge and watched him take that long, blissful fall.

He thrust his hips sharply and groaned as his cock pulsed. I swallowed his spending and rubbed his erection until the last spasm passed through it. Then I sat back on my heels and studied every bare inch of the man. I wished I'd had him take off his shirt. Was it too late now to strip him completely and do more things with his handsome body? No. For I believed once that smile faded from his lips and he came back to himself, this miraculous moment would be over. Doubt and shame would flood back in, and he'd flee from me. I'd had a few of his ilk before and knew how difficult it was for them to let go of their notions about what a man must never do.

But Richard—not Sir Richard now, at least not in my mind—surprised me.

His eyes flickered open, and he looked down upon me at his feet. He held out a hand to pull me up, and though he was still drunk, he was able to without toppling over.

We faced each other in silence for several moments. The usual light comments that came easily to my tongue were absent. For once, I didn't know what to say. I expected him to put his cock away, straighten his clothes, and leave, later pretending as if none of this had happened—until next time his need grew too urgent.

Instead, he pulled me close with the hand that still clutched mine and held me against him. I relaxed into strong arms and listened to his voice rumble in his chest when he spoke. "Let me do the same for you. I want to."

I stepped away while Richard fastened his trousers. He motioned me to sit in the front pew. I obeyed and waited, handing control over to him.

He dropped heavily to his knees in front of me like a suitor about to propose, and for several seconds, simply looked at me as though deciding how to proceed. My cock helpfully tented the fabric of my nightshirt to make certain he could see it there. Richard bit his lower lip and tentatively reached toward the hem of my shirt.

"You haven't done this before," I said.

He shook his head. "Not this. Other things."

With who? I wondered, but this wasn't the time to pry out more secrets.

"No hurry. You don't have to do anything you don't wish to." I stroked back a lock of hair that had fallen over his glazed eyes, but the gesture felt too intimate—somehow more than having his cock in my mouth.

"But I *do* wish to," he hastened to answer with a drunkard's effusive desire to make himself understood. "I've dreamed of this, perhaps since I first saw you."

I preened at the compliment. Good to know I wasn't the only one who'd felt a flare of attraction that day.

Richard rested a hand on my thigh, bunching up the fabric of the nightshirt, then smoothing it again. "I apologize for before." He gazed at his own hand rather than look into my eyes. "I tried to force you. That's not my nature. It was as if something possessed me." He glanced at me with a rueful smile. "Perhaps nearly an entire flask of whisky."

I smiled back. "I don't mind a little roughness now and again. And I like being fucked in the arse. But it goes more smoothly with some lubrication."

He flinched when I said *fucked* and swallowed hard at the word *lubrication*. "I haven't done that before either," he admitted softly.

Just what in the hell *had* he done and with whom? My cat was dying of curiosity, but I knew it would be better to let Richard confess on his own. Though he knelt at my knee like a penitent, I was not his priest to order up five Hail Marys and an Act of Contrition, nor was he a Catholic, prone to the barter of prayers for grace.

Richard kept reflexively bunching and smoothing my nightshirt against my leg. The repetitious tickle of fabric was more erotic than if he'd gone straight for my goods. My cock pulsed each time he smoothed the cotton against my bare skin.

I studied his frowning face and realized I no longer thought of Allinson as in a position of authority over me. I was the one with experience. He was the novice to be tutored. And he was nervous.

"Listen, you can't get it wrong. I'll appreciate anything you do, trust me. Just think about what you would enjoy and do that," I suggested.

He slid the nightshirt up a few more inches, baring my pale, hairy legs. He licked his lips, and I swallowed hard. My cock tensed almost painfully, unwilling to wait much longer for the touching to begin.

"Will it help if I close my eyes and don't watch you?" I asked.

He nodded, and that lock of hair fell over his forehead again. I left it there this time, because he looked so adorable that way.

I leaned back, arms stretched along the top of the pew, and closed my eyes. Thinking of all the people who'd come here to worship God added an extra twist of forbidden pleasure to what we were doing. Fantasies of lewd public displays before an audience drove my urgency to a new level. And then, at last, Richard's hands slid up my thighs, pushing the nightshirt higher and higher until cool air brushed my groin.

My cock jutted forward, waiting, waiting, waiting… Fingers tickled the tender flesh of my inner thighs, making me shiver, and then a large, warm hand circled my staff and gripped it. I exhaled in relief. This was what I'd craved for days—a release of tension beyond what I gave myself during private moments, a physical connection with this man, whom I desired with an unreasonable intensity.

As warm breath tickled my intimate flesh, followed by the scouring heat of Richard's mouth, I gripped the back of that pew hard to keep from being utterly swept away. Hot, wet, deeper and deeper he engulfed me. I tried to distance myself from that point of contact lest I immediately give in to pleasure.

Richard's mouth drew away, leaving my cock damp and chilled. "Wasn't that right? You're frowning."

I rocked my hips forward to beg for more. "You're doing wonderfully. Carry on, please. I'm just trying to keep from coming in your face."

A small "Oh" and then more heat and slippery wetness surrounded me. Now he sucked, a bit sloppily but oh so endearingly eager. Richard sucked so hard and rubbed my root so firmly, I thought he'd milk me dry. I groaned and shifted on the hard wooden bench, inhaling sour alcohol and pipe smoke and a faint whiff of burning candle wax. The darkness behind my closed eyes intensified every scent, every sensation, but I needed more.

I wanted not only to feel but to *see* Sir Richard Allinson sucking me off like a Spitalfields molly. Through my eyelashes, I watched his handsome head bob up and down, his hollowed cheeks and lips stretched around my girth. What a gloriously perverse and thrilling sight. Relaxing against the hard bench, I felt like a pasha accepting the succor of his servant.

Richard's fist moved briskly as he massaged me for several minutes, and he never flagged in his slurping and sucking. The tension in my balls grew tighter and then, all in a moment, my excitement became too great to contain. I moaned louder and thrust forward so my cock nearly choked him. My cry of release echoed through the chapel.

I hadn't warned Richard it was coming, so he didn't pull off but swallowed every drop. He waited for the last convulsion to pass through me before letting my cock slip from between his glistening lips. He drew away, wiping his mouth on the back of his hand, and looked up at me with *have I satisfied you?* eyes.

"That was perfect," I commended my pupil. "You did it just right."

I drew my nightshirt back down my legs, thinking surely now would be the end. Richard's haze from all that liquor had begun to subside. His desires had been fulfilled. Now he would seek an escape.

But again he surprised me. He sat back on the floor, drew his knees up and wrapped his arms around them, as if he wanted to chat awhile.

I was up for talking any time anywhere. "Tell me about this man you were with before."

He rested his chin on his knees, appearing more boyish than ever. "Not only one. I dallied with a few fellows at boarding school, mutual rub offs in the study rooms, no more than that. After I married Lavinia, I vowed to put such youthful nonsense behind me. But then sometimes, when I did business in another city, I would go to certain places and came very close to falling. I began to understand the schoolboy 'nonsense' wasn't anything I'd outgrow. That desire would be a part of me forever. I couldn't fight it or change it, and no matter how much I cared for my wife, I never felt true passion for her."

I nodded. I'd come to that understanding much earlier in my life, but it had still been something of a revelation.

"Each time I made eye contact with some stranger and almost went off with him, I'd stopped myself from following through. And every near encounter only stoked my craving, and my private fantasies. But my respect for Lavinia was too great to treat her that way. I decided it would be better to remain celibate than indulge in vice."

"And you succeeded for a long time, until…"

He exhaled softly. "Until…"

I leaned forward to rest my arms against my knees and studied the emotions passing over Richard's expressive face, each telling part of the story: desire, guilt, passion, shame, sorrow. "My special man was named Sylvester Leighton. Who was yours?"

He remained silent for so long I thought he might not answer, but finally he spoke. "Jerry Eccleston, the former groom. I'd already pared the stable down to a few mounts, mostly manageable by a single head groom. But I enjoyed helping him exercise the horses, taking long rides across the countryside. We talked a bit and then a little more, at first about horses or the weather, but later about life, our thoughts about the world…and other things. With every conversation I grew more…"

This time Richard didn't resume his train of thought. He didn't need to say he'd fallen in love. I could see that plainly on his face, and I felt a mad stab of jealousy for the horseman who'd ridden off with Richard's heart. I'd never felt anything close to what I'd call love, not even with my dear Sylvester. I'd cared for the man, yes, admired, respected, and learned from him. I wouldn't have become who I was without his kindness and generosity. But *love*? That was something else entirely.

Richard rubbed a hand over his face. "Liquor loosens my tongue. I've spoken too much." He climbed to his feet, signaling our time was over.

Disappointment sheared through me. Why didn't *I* have a say as to when we were finished talking? But I rose also, prepared to follow him from the room.

He picked up the candle from the altar, the only light he'd brought with him, then paused. "I thank you for tonight, but it mustn't happen again."

"Yes, sir. I understand." Though I didn't really. His wife was dead now. Why did he continue to hold back from what he craved? Was it some form of self-punishment? No one but he and I would be any the wiser.

But it wasn't my place to bring up such thoughts. By the time we walked from the room, we'd resumed our proper roles as master and servant.

CHAPTER 14

One breathtaking, unbelievable night with Richard wasn't nearly enough. I suspected he felt the same. Despite what he'd said, I felt fairly confident we would come together again. Meanwhile, that passionate event didn't change the routine of my days, though I approached my duties with renewed purpose. If I couldn't influence the stubborn Sir Richard to believe he wasn't responsible for his wife's suicide, I might at least reach his sons. I was determined to make some impact on this family and help them heal.

Whitney and Clive as a single unit were impossible to breach. The boys would confide in no one but each other. However, I perceived Whit was the weaker link. He was the first to soften toward me, and I believed he liked me. If I could get him away from Clive's influence for a time, he might crack and release the infection of blame that tormented both him and his brother.

While I waited for the right opportunity to arise, I often thought about Lavinia Allinson, wife, mother, ghostly spirit. I considered what I'd learned of her death, but also recalled the dark entity in Clive's drawings and Tom's depictions of evil. Those artistic renderings suggested a malevolent presence, perhaps the ghost of a long-dead killer, if Tom's recent drawing was to be believed. Some sinister being bided its time like a spider in a web, waiting to trap its victim. I felt this in my very bones.

I recalled what my friend Madame Alijeva, aka Mrs. Glass, a spiritualist medium, had once told me. The tiny wren of a woman's ability to channel the dead was as false as the color of her red hair. She affected the style of a mystic, wearing embroidered robes and a feathered turban, arms jangling with bracelets, loops of glass beads around her neck. Her Russian accent added an air of gravity and believability to her pronouncements, though I knew she was a second-generation Londoner and the widow of a middle-class merchant rather than Russian nobility as she claimed for her customers.

"Don't you feel bad, taking their money?" I'd once asked after helping her with one of her séances.

"Not at all." Madame dabbed at her teary eyes with a lace-trimmed handkerchief. "They got what they wanted…piz."

I smiled at her pronunciation of *peace*, which came out sounding like *piss*, a much better description of her charade.

"Piz of mind I give them. It is worth the price, you see?"

I sat back in my chair in her stuffy parlor, resting a hand on the table between us that had been rocking and floating not too long before. "I see it's a pack of lies, all this talk about the other side and piercing the veil."

"No, no, no." She waved her beringed hands. "Not lies." She clapped a hand to her chest. "*I* may not be condueet to spirits, but they exeest. I know thees. I have seen with my own two eyes." She pointed at her vivid blue orbs.

"What have you seen?"

"You listen. When I was girl in St. Petersburg…"

"Madame, you never lived in St. Petersburg."

She shrugged. "All right, Bethnal Green at home of my aunt. She would tell me stories from the Motherland. Aunt Sonia had visions, could see and talk to spirits. She told me some are lost, wandering, not able to…to…" She clutched her hands and shook them. "Let go, *da?*"

I nodded. "Unfinished business. Others linger because their lives were ended violently and abruptly. I've heard the pitch."

"Mr. Knows-it-all," Alijeva scoffed. "You know about demons? Dark, evil spirits that feed off emotions of the living? You know *that?*"

"I don't believe in hauntings *or* demons." I lied a bit, because a superstitious streak made the hair on my neck prickle at the mere mention of demonic forces.

"Beliv. Not beliv. Don't matter. This things exeest. My aunt experience many times both in Russia and here."

I sat forward on my chair, elbows on the table. "What about you? You said you had an eyewitness account?"

"Ah, yes." Tears shone again, making her eyes two watery pools. The ease with which she conjured tears for her clients made me generally doubt her emotions. Yet this time she appeared sincere.

"I sat at my mama's kitchen table, cutting paper doilies to sell at market. I look up, and there she is. My Aunt Sonia." Madame waved her hands. "I ask why she come. To see Mama? She look at me with eyes like burning coal." Another dramatic pointing gesture at her eyes. "Then she walk out of room. I get up to follow her and she is—*poof*—gone."

Despite my professed disbelief, a shiver tickled my spine. "Let me guess. You learned your aunt had died that day."

Alijeva stabbed the air with her finger. "Not only that day but that. Very. Minute!"

"A compelling story." *If it was true*, I'd thought at the time.

Looking back at the conversation with Madame Alijeva, I believed there was a core of truth in what she said. If the odd occurrences I'd experienced at Allinson Hall—the wisp of blue, the sobbing and whispers, the sorrow infiltrating my spirit—weren't signs of dead Lavinia's energy haunting the place, I didn't know what else they could be. Might the disturbingly malicious other presence I'd felt be one of Madame Alijeva's purported demons? If it was, what did it want, and could I expel it?

I recalled another friend's tale about a lighthouse keeper who'd killed his entire family and whose evil still supposedly haunted the lighthouse. A family later tried to live there and nearly came to the same fate when the father was possessed by the evil spirit. Or so the story went.

Whether the entity was a killer's ghost or demonic force, I needed to learn more about the history of the Hall, a daunting task, for generations had lived there and any horrific act would have been hushed up much like Lavinia Allinson's suicide. I could hardly expect to find a volume of family history to spell things out for me. And did it matter? Maybe instead I should search for a book about expelling ghosts and demons. Either way, I needed to make another trip to the library.

I came to this conclusion one afternoon when the boys and I were on break from lessons. I'd left the twins playing a game of cards while I used the water closet and sat there musing possible outcomes if I should happen to meet Richard in the library.

When I returned to the schoolroom, Clive played solitaire at the table and Whit was gone.

"Where's your brother?" I asked. It was rare to see one without the other, and since I'd just come from the WC, I knew Whit wasn't there.

Clive stopped flipping cards long enough to nod toward the door. I was left to figure out what that meant. Irritation sizzled through me. I wondered if it might prove useful to simply demand Clive stop being a little jackass and use words. Perhaps coddling his muteness was the wrong thing to do.

But I wasn't quite ready to get stern with him, so I left the room and went to the boys' bedroom. There I found Whit stretched out on his bed on top of the covers, a shaft of sunlight from the window making his blond hair glow. He quickly snatched his thumb from his mouth when I entered.

"Not feeling well?" I leaned over to touch his forehead, which was warm.

He nodded.

I sat on the edge of the bed. "What's wrong?"

"My stomach." He rested a hand on it.

"Sorry to hear it. Maybe something you ate at lunch. Cook's awful soup, perhaps." I smiled. "Get some rest. If you don't feel better in a bit, I'll see about sending for the doctor."

He shook his head. "No! Not the doctor."

I thought of the last time he'd probably seen the man, on the occasion of his mother's death. "He might prescribe a tonic to help you feel better," I pointed out.

"I'm not sick," Whit protested.

"Tell you what. I'll have Cook make you custard. That's the thing for a bad stomach. My mum used to treat us to custard when we were sick—if there were eggs or sugar to be had."

Whit rubbed his flushed cheek. I rose and pulled the curtain to shelter him from the bright sunbeam.

"I miss my mum." His whisper might've been meant for himself.

I returned to sit beside him again and hold his small hand. "You've had a great loss. After my pa and sisters and brother died, nothing felt right for a very long time." No point in telling him they'd never been right again, not for my grieving mother or Cynthia or me. "Tell me about your mum. I've seen her portrait in your father's study. She was a beautiful lady."

Whit remained quiet for a moment, then confided, "She told us stories and sometimes played Pachisi with us, when she wasn't busy resting." He thought a moment. "And when we were sick, she'd sing a special song to make us feel better."

I smiled. "What song is that?"

"Lullay, my liking, my dear one…" Whit frowned. "I don't know the words anymore."

"I know it." I recalled the tune if not the lyrics of the medieval Christmas song, and I began to sing. "Lullay, mine liking, my dear son, mine sweeting. Lullay, my dear heart, mine own dear darling."

Whit's eyes brightened. "Yes! Like that."

And then, although I hadn't heard my own mum sing it in years, it was as if she whispered the words straight into my ear.

"I saw a fair maiden, sittin' and singin'. She lulled a little child, a sweet lording. The eternal lord is that, who maketh all things. Of all lords he is Lord. Of all kings, he is King."

I sang straight through several verses, and when I was finished, Whit rewarded me with one of his rare smiles.

I smiled back, thinking how much sweeter children were when sickness laid them low. He was such a pathetic little thing that I leaned in and gave him a kiss on the forehead before I rose to leave. "Sleep now. I'll be back later with custard as I promised."

Before I made it to the door, Whit called after me. "Mr. Cowrie."

I turned. "Yes?"

"I'm sorry for playing tricks on you before."

I grinned. "That's all right. I played many a prank myself as a lad. I'll tell you about them sometime, so long as you promise not to use them on anyone else."

"No," Whit said. "Not even on Smithers."

When I was almost out the door, his voice floated after me again.

"I like you, Mr. Cowrie. I don't care what Clive thinks."

I closed the door behind me and shook my head. Clive. He was a bigger nut to crack than his brother, and no wonder, after what he'd seen. Perhaps my divide-and-conquer strategy might work with him now.

I headed back to the schoolroom, but it was empty. The little squirrel had scampered off to wherever he and Whit went when they weren't able to go to their garden hideaway.

With a little free time on my hands, I decided to go to the library and search for books, either occult or family histories. I was disappointed to find the large room vacant, but realized it was for the best as I could search without interruption.

I easily found the family Bible listing generations of Allinsons right back to their origins. But the long roll of names with birth and death dates informed me of nothing. There was Richard Gerard Allinson. Thirty-three according to his birth date, though his careworn face added a half-dozen years. I traced a fingertip over *Lavinia Allinson, nee Stewart. Born 1865. Died 1892.* Not yet thirty, the poor sad soul. And there were the twins, Clive Bernard and Whitney Joseph, written in Richard's bold cursive.

One last time I scanned the genealogical tree, trying to pluck something fruitful from its branches. But it told me no stories. I closed the Bible and began to search the rest of the library, starting with the dustiest tomes on the top shelves, which required a ladder to reach. Surely any occult books would be hidden there.

If I'd hoped to uncover a fool's guide to exorcism or some handwritten volume containing all the shocking truths about the Allinson family, I was disappointed. Instead, I merely got dirtier and thirstier as I glanced at one book after another, getting distracted and reading passages in some.

I was wiping a spider web from my face when a voice came from below.

"May I help you find something, Mr. Cowrie?"

My foot slipped, and I went down a few rungs on the narrow ladder before catching myself. At the same time, hands gripped my waist until I'd regained my balance. Those strong hands held me for several moments before letting go.

"Just poking around in these older books." I climbed the rest of the way down the ladder and faced Sir Richard. "Good afternoon, sir."

He smiled, an honest, genuine, beautiful smile. "Good afternoon."

We both stood grinning at each other. Richard reached out to brush his fingers through my hair, and I went instantly hard.

He showed me what he'd retrieved from my hair. "Cobweb. Not enough maids to clean thoroughly."

"Ah." I stared at the white strands on his fingers that reminded me of something else white and sticky.

Finally, Richard cleared his throat. "What book are you searching for?"

"Nothing in particular. I was merely curious what sort of books one might hide away on the very top shelf. Nothing nearly as offensive as I'd hoped to find," I joked.

"We Allinsons are a dull lot. I couldn't imagine some great-grandfather stocking the library with a secret collection of pornography." His tiny smile put me at ease. It was the first glimmer I'd seen of the man Richard might be when not weighed down by guilt and sadness.

He stood so near me, I smelled the pipe he must have just put out. Such a rich tobacco aroma, it made me want to grab the lapels of his coat, lean in, and simply inhale. Silence fell but for the slight creaking of the wood floor and the ticking of the mantel clock.

Magnetics at work again, my body inevitably inclined toward

Richard, and he bowed his head slightly toward me. We vibrated on the edge of possibility. My mouth ached for a kiss, and my body for much more than that.

A book I'd placed nowhere near the edge of the shelf suddenly tumbled from high above to hit me on the head with a sharp blow.

Help them! the familiar inner directive came.

Yes, Lavinia. Your message from beyond the veil is received loud and clear, you annoying bint.

I rubbed my injured cranium and bent to pick up the book at the same time Richard stooped for it. Our heads cracked together, and I saw stars. But after recovering from the pain, I began to laugh. Miracle of miracles, Richard did too.

We squatted on the floor, chuckling like fools, and I thought I'd never heard music as sweet as this man's laughter, perhaps because it was so hard-won. Hell, if I'd known pratfalls made Richard laugh like that, I'd have entertained him with pants-falling-down buffoonery before now.

When I'd caught my breath and rose with the book in hand, I addressed him seriously. "Sir, I should tell you Whitney is feeling poorly today."

His lingering smile vanished. "He's sick?"

"A stomach ache and slight fever. Likely not worth a doctor's visit, although if he doesn't improve by tomorrow…" I shrugged. "But the poor little fellow's quite wretched. A visit from you would cheer him up."

Richard continued to frown. "I'm not so certain it would."

"It *would*." I leveled my sternest schoolteacher glare at him, the one I'd been perfecting on Whit and Clive for all the good it did in getting them to obey me. "You must go to him. It's long past time you cleared the air with both boys."

He swiped a hand over his chin. "I do check on the twins, you know. Many nights when they're sleeping, I look in on them."

Which explained what he'd been doing near my room the other night. Not coming to see me at all, but watching over his sons.

"Fat lot of good that does when they don't even know you're there." I spoke boldly, no longer feigning deference. "They must be shown you care, *and* you must reassure them the loss of their mother is not your fault—even if you don't believe it yourself." *There, Lavinia! I batted for our side. Let's see if I score a point.*

The master of the house stared at me as if unable to believe my presumption. "You are far too outspoken and very confident in your opinions, Cowrie. Hardly the model employee. In fact, I believe you have no experience in a household such as this, have you? No teaching experience at all. I had my agent in London look into your references, and they do not bear close scrutiny."

My bravado burst like a popped balloon, and fear rushed out. I'd been caught. Foolish to believe I could pull off this charade for long. Allinson would have the law on me for fraud. And yet, he'd learned this fact and said nothing before now.

"When did you know?" I asked, not trying to deny the truth.

"The other night..." He didn't have to say which one. "Your accent made your story of being an impoverished gentleman questionable. I wired my man to check into your credentials more thoroughly, a task I should've performed before hiring you. I was so grateful to have any response to my advertisement, I'll admit I was less than particular."

"And now that you've found out?" My heart fired off bursts of uneven scattershot beats as I waited to learn my fate.

He cocked his head quizzically. "What *have* I discovered? Who are you really, Graham Cowrie? Tell me. For my agent was able to find nothing about you at all."

I held the book clutched to my chest like a protective breastplate. This day had taken a most unexpected turn. I had no idea how it would end, but I had to tell the truth.

"I worked as a print typesetter and saw your advertisement. I'd been pondering ways to advance myself in the world, and the situation seemed a tailor-made opportunity to gain prestigious experience for my résumé."

Richard stood with arms folded, leaning back against a bookcase. "This seemed like a good idea to you, to falsify references and pretend to a skill you don't possess?"

"Well, I *have* taught a few other blokes to read. I figured I was well-educated enough to impart knowledge to a couple of tykes." I gauged Richard's reaction. He seemed more gobsmacked than angry at my cheek. Did I actually detect a twinkle in his dark eyes?

"How did you gain this education? What is your background?"

No more hiding behind prevarications or half truths. He'd have it all from me. I drew a breath.

"My name, once upon a time, was Joe Green, son of a bricklayer and a washerwoman, but I've been Graham Cowrie for a number of years now. The gentleman I told you was a particular friend of mine, Sylvester Leighton, took me in when I was a youth. He taught me manners, culture, and refinement and furthered my education in every way." I recalled my mentor Leighton with bittersweet regret. "But, as happens, he lost interest in me over time and went in search of a fresher bud for his lapel."

"Mm." Richard gave a small grunt either of understanding or sympathy, perhaps both.

I shrugged to show the abandonment hadn't hurt me, although when Leighton first tossed me to the winds, it had felt like the end of the world.

"Armed with my education and improved accent, guv'nor, and with a parting reference letter from Leighton, I secured the job at the printing press. I toiled there for a couple of years with no seeming chance for advancement, which led me to…" I extended a hand, indicating the room where we stood. "I'm sorry I lied to you, but not sorry I took this position, for I've grown exceedingly fond of both Whit and Clive." I ducked my head and coyly looked at Richard from beneath my eyebrows. "Not to mention the master of the house."

Sir Richard cupped his chin in hand, covering his mouth—maybe to hide a smile?—and shook his head. He withdrew his hand to speak. "You are outrageous, Graham Cowrie. I ought to fire you on the spot. I *ought* to send for the constable and have you arrested."

"But you won't?" I suggested hopefully.

"You know I won't, cheeky bugger." He stepped away from the shelves. One step toward me that made my pulse quicken. I was positive he was going to grab me and kiss me.

"I'm not sure what I'll do about you," he continued. "But I do know that right now I must go and see my sick son."

I exhaled my disappointment. "Yes, of course."

Allinson brushed past me, our shoulders bumping, and I almost reached for his hand, pulled him to a halt and into my arms. But I'd probably pushed my luck as far as I dared already today.

I watched him leave before climbing the ladder to reshelf Lavinia's book grenade. Maybe it had fallen all by itself. I tried to believe that, but it was no longer possible to overlook all the strange occurrences adding up. And I *really* couldn't ignore the still small voice of an anxious mother in my head.

Help them. Heal them. Give them love.

Check. Check. And check, I promised her.

CHAPTER 15

Wanting to give Richard time alone with his sons, I decided not to head straight back up to the children's rooms in the house. I took a moment to write a letter to Madame Alijeva, outlining what I'd been experiencing and asking her advice, which I put with the outgoing post. Then I decided a breath of air to clear the dust from my nose, the lust haze from my body, and the haunting voice from my head was what I needed.

As I passed the kitchen, I offered a chipper hello to dour Cook and her shrinking scullery maid, whose name I still hadn't learned.

I went out a side door into the kitchen garden, which would be redolent of herbs in summer but was now as crusty and dead as the rest of the gardens. Tom sat on a bench in a corner protected from the breeze, polishing shoes.

"Hello there," I greeted him and sat on a low stone wall to soak up the few weak sunbeams. I watched his precise movements with the blacking brush and the polishing rag. He currently worked on a pair of Richard's shoes, which I couldn't see without thinking of the man's feet, his large, well-proportioned body, his sculpted features, his…everything.

I shook off my rising interest and focused on Tom's homely face, the low forehead and off-kilter features and his intense concentration on his task. During our evening sessions as I'd worked on my story while Tom drew or painted, I'd tried repeatedly to get him to talk to me, and sometimes he'd spoken a few words. Since I knew he was one of the few people aware of the true cause of Lavinia's death, I decided to pry for more details.

"Tommy," I said.

His gaze flicked up to meet mine.

I approached the topic sideways. "What do you know about the tower room? I've seen your drawings, the dark thing you sometimes paint, that scene with the killer. Can you tell me more?"

He returned his gaze to the shoes, but his buffing brush moved slowly.

"Please, Tommy, I'll believe whatever you say. Something is wrong in this house. I want to help make things better if I can," I told him truthfully.

More silence followed. I watched a beetle scuttle across the flagstones and into a crack which must be its home.

"Old Grandda told a tale 'bout a monster in man's skin." Tom's unexpectedly deep and mature voice startled me. This was the longest sentence he'd yet spoken. I didn't look at him for fear of frightening him back into muteness.

"How long ago?" I dared to ask. "What did the man do?"

"Old Da's great-grandda worked here like me. He knew the truth."

Several generations could mean over a hundred years ago or more. "Go on," I prodded gently. "I'm listening."

"Never tell outsiders, Old Da said."

"I won't repeat a word to anyone. But there's a time for secrets to come out. If Whit and Clive are in any real danger, I need to know." I could hardly believe I was suggesting some evil ghost had any power over the living.

Tom stopped buffing shoes to stare at me intensely. Whatever people thought about his mental capacity, there was a light on inside. And then he began to recite a story it seemed he'd heard many times.

"Young master was cruel. Tore up and killed animals as a lad. Servants knew." Tom gazed at his polishing rag as if seeing this long-ago story unfold. "Later, some people went missing—a milkmaid herdin' cows, a woman folks said likely drowned. But no bodies and no one thinkin' it be a killer—till it kept happenin' over a few years. Then folks got scared and called him the Stealer."

I leaned forward, as chilled as if there were no sunshine warming my back. I'd been close by when the Ripper haunted Whitechapel, and I'd never forget the terror that galvanized everyone. Though, in some people's eyes, he'd "merely" killed prostitutes—the dregs of the city—those of us living near the district felt every murder as a personal assault.

"How did they catch him? Or was he never discovered?"

Tom nodded. "Oh, aye."

"Tell me," I whispered, eager to know and not wanting to hear at the same time.

"A maid here disappeared, and they thought she'd run off. Except she left all her things." Tom gave me a look, making sure I got the point.

"Why would the killer strike close to home after being careful for so long?" I wondered aloud. "Did she stumble across something she shouldn't have seen? Or maybe he thrived on risking bigger stakes to achieve his thrill. I've read such killers feel invincible and cleverer than everyone else."

My reading of Conan Doyle's detective novels for pleasure may have proved instructional after all. What would Sherlock Holmes do with the case of a haunted tower room? Likely find a very human and non-otherworldly explanation for it.

"How was he finally caught?" I asked.

"People heard quiet screamin' and cryin' from the walls and feared a ghost. But Great-Great-Grandda searched out the noise."

"Coming from the tower," I guessed. My heart was in my mouth with fear for a maid who'd faced death so long ago. "Did he get there in time?"

Tom dipped the blacking brush and rubbed thoughtfully at a scuff on the toe of Richard's boot. "The tower was locked. Great-Grandda went to Allinson for the key."

"Wait. I thought Allinson was the killer."

"*Young* master, the son. Had her strung up by a rope and did things to her with a knife." Tom crossed himself and spit over one shoulder to ward off the devil.

"Was she dead when they got there?" I asked.

"Near to. Young master had a knife, but his father had a sword. He said…" Tom quoted exactly as Old Da must have told it. "'Curse you. You are no son of mine, you insane bastard. The world will be well rid of you,' and stabbed him through."

"Did the girl survive?"

Tom shook his head. "The master cut her down and finished her with the bloody sword. Great-Grandda got rid of the bodies and swore silence, said our family is cursed if the vow be broken."

The entire story sounded like a melodrama. If I hadn't spent a few minutes up in that haunted tower, I could hardly have believed it. But as it was, every bit of the horrific tale rang true.

"Thank you for trusting me with the story, Tom." Although now that I knew it, I had no idea what to do about it. One violent crime or more had occurred in the tower. Such an event would surely be enough to anchor the dead to this world, reliving the ordeal. What could one do to get rid of spirits infesting a house? And could they actually harm the living?

"Evil lives in the tower," Tom said suddenly. "It killed Mrs. Allinson."

"How?" I considered the suicide I wasn't supposed to know about, a death that mirrored the hanging in his story.

"Sometimes it whispers." He touched his ear and glanced at the house looming behind him.

I knew he didn't mean a literal voice but the hopeless gloom that sometimes invaded my soul. So, I wasn't the only one. And Lavinia's crushing depression might have come from outside her as well.

"I watch the boys so they don't come to harm," Tom confessed.

"I'll keep watch with you." I rose from my seat on the stone wall and clapped him on the shoulder. "We'll be vigilant, you and I, and make certain no harm comes to anyone in the house on our watch."

Bravely said, though I had no idea how to protect anyone. If such spirits fed off turbulent human emotion, this one surely gathered strength from Clive's anger, the Allinson family's grief, and perhaps from the simmering passion between me and Richard. Now all it needed was a suggestible mind to corrupt. I was determined I wouldn't allow those insidious feelings of despair to creep inside me again.

CHAPTER 16

I would love to have been a fly on the wall to witness the meeting of Richard and his sons. As it was, I was merely privy to the result, which was Whit displaying a cheerier disposition and Clive seemingly angrier and more aloof than ever. I never knew what all had transpired, if Richard had been unable to get Clive to listen to him or if he'd even tried. But from that afternoon on, it was obvious a rift had formed between the twins, their inseparable bond coming unraveled at the seams.

Over the next days, the more Whit talked to me, answered my questions during lessons, or made little jokes and laughed about some silly nonsense I'd invented, the more sullen Clive became. Whitney no longer spoke for his brother. Despite my ongoing efforts to draw responses from Clive, I still couldn't get the dour lad to speak a word. I had no idea how to reach him, and he almost seemed worse than when I'd first met him.

For the rest of that week, I had no brushes with Allinson. Maybe he was still considering everything he'd learned about me. Maybe I'd still find myself out on my ear. But I would've at least expected him to check in with me about the boys. Not that he owed me that. He was the boss. I was hired help. Why did I have so much trouble remembering my place?

I was relieved to have another half day off to escape the insular environment of the Hall. I didn't have time to walk to the village and back, but was able to catch a ride with Drover. Some of the same customers nursed mugs of ale at the pub. I also made new acquaintances, all of whom seemed welcoming and happy to stand a round. As a result, Drover had to support my drunken weight on the way to the wagon for our return home. I slung an arm around his shoulders and tried to get him to sing along with me. He wouldn't.

I drowsed with my chin bobbing against my chest, and Drover had to pull over twice to let me say good-bye to all the ale I'd drunk. Back in the stable yard, he prodded me awake, and I staggered indoors, happily without running into Smithers or anyone else on the way to my room. I passed out on top of my bed with shoes and coat still on.

Late that night, I awoke with a heavy weight bearing me down into the mattress, compressing my chest so I could only breathe in shallow gasps. I couldn't lift my arms to push the thing off me. I tried to roll my body out from under it, but I might as well have been in a straitjacket and tied to the bed. I'd once thought Allinson Hall had the grim air of a lunatic asylum. Now it felt as if I were an inmate. Worst of all, I couldn't seem to pry my eyes open to *see* what held me down.

I remained locked in silent, motionless battle with my attacker for what felt like hours, though I had no true knowledge of the passage of time. I experienced a sensation of utter defenselessness and felt I fought against something truly evil that would never release me.

This is how it ends. The crystal-clear thought dropped into my mind. *This is how you leave the world.* Damned if I would! I pushed back with all my strength, and I don't mean physically but with the power of my will.

Abruptly, I broke through, jerked awake, and sat up, gasping for air. I celebrated the simple joy of being able to move my limbs and body by jumping out of bed. I tore off the overcoat I still wore and pulled off my shoes, then took off my clothes for good measure. My body was drenched with sweat from the struggle.

What struggle? It was only a dream, I assured myself as I splashed water on my face and chest and drank deeply straight from the pitcher. But the experience had certainly felt real and life threatening. If I was accepting the premise that spirits existed, it wasn't a stretch to assume I'd been attacked by the vile killer who refused to leave this house. If his evil energy could attack me this way, what might he try with the boys and, again, what could I do to prevent it?

I changed into clean clothes and went to look in on Clive and Whitney—both sound asleep, each in his own bed. I wanted to sit in a chair in their room and simply watch over them, but their sleep appeared peaceful and their breathing calm and regular.

After a few moments, I went downstairs and let myself out into the garden, where I strolled for a while before sitting on a stone bench to watch the sky lighten from gray to rose to orange. Even the worst fears may fade to mere shadows in the brightness of a new day.

I returned to the house, starving for breakfast and feeling quite myself again. I would figure out some way to quell the demon in the tower even if I had to get hold of goddamn holy water and perform invented exorcism rites myself. I wondered if Madame Alijeva had received my letter yet and what she might write in return.

Just then I met Richard coming down to breakfast as I was about to head upstairs. He paused a few steps above me so I looked up to meet his gaze.

"Good morning, Cowrie."

"Good morning, sir." There was so much I wanted to discuss with him, these polite pleasantries annoyed me. But this wasn't the time or place for a more personal talk.

"Back from an early morning walk?"

"Yes," I replied.

"Well…" Richard continued down the stairs but paused in front of me. "I want to thank you."

"Oh…" I didn't know what to say, *No thanks needed* or *For what?* Both were disingenuous, for I knew why he thanked me and thought I deserved it for pushing him to repair broken family bonds. "I'm glad you spoke with the boys."

"Only Whitney. Clive was nowhere to be found."

"He's hard to pin down, that one." I remembered *why* Clive was temperamental, the burden of the secret he carried. But Whit likely knew the same secret and wasn't nearly as angry. The twins looked alike but underneath were as different as could be.

"When you have the time, sir, there are a few matters I'd like to discuss," I said.

"Later this afternoon you may come to my study."

Richard continued on without looking at me again, perhaps attempting to keep our interaction suitably professional.

God knew every time we spent more than a few minutes together behind closed doors, professionalism slipped and intimacy took over. And it wasn't merely base animal hunger, but a connection of minds that put us on equal footing. Under the right set of circumstances, I could enjoy spending much more time in Richard Allinson's company. There were many facets of the man yet to uncover. Our shared love of reading alone would keep us talking for hours. Sex could fill much of the rest of the time.

But that dream wouldn't happen. Though I was amenable to an arrangement of nightly visits when I wasn't occupied with my students, Richard would never give in to temptation without regretting it afterward. He was too mired in guilt and doubt and perhaps disgust for his perverse desires. However, I had to admit he'd sounded more regretful about cheating on his wife than repulsed by who he'd done it with. I didn't really get the sense of a man who despised his man-loving side. Maybe there *was* room in him for change given time.

And we had many long, shut-in months of winter ahead of us.

The morning was fine and sunny, but, from my window, I saw clouds looming on the horizon. I decided to take advantage of good weather while I was able and get the boys outdoors. After breakfast, we dressed in coats, hats, boots, and gloves and braved the frigid temperature in order to get some sun on our faces.

I engaged them in a game that mingled elements of tag with hide-and-seek and even got sour-puss Clive running around the paths in the garden. His mood seemed to have lifted with the sunshine. I couldn't help but wonder if much of his gloom was due to the influence of the house—or more precisely, the entity *in* the house.

On my turn as it, I chased Whit and cornered him by the vine-covered wall of the hidden garden. I tagged him. After he'd caught his breath, he said, "I want to show you something, Mr. Cowrie."

"Very well."

I expected him to pull something from his pocket, a boyish treasure of a shiny stone or bird feather, but instead he beckoned me. "Come on."

After a few steps, I knew where Whit was leading me. He pulled aside a curtain of vines to reveal the gap in the wall and gazed up at me with eyes as solemn as his father's, except blue instead of dark.

"This is a special place. Only Clive and I come here. You can't talk about it to anyone."

I nodded, keeping my expression equally serious. I was being inducted into the twins' secret society, allowed into their private sanctuary.

"I understand," I replied. "Besides, who would I tell? Smithers?"

I smiled, and Whit smiled back.

Before entering, I paused. "What about Clive? Is it all right with him you're bringing me here?"

Whit shrugged, and as if summoned by the mention of his name, Clive came running from wherever he'd been hiding. He planted himself between me and the entrance to the enclosed garden. As usual, he didn't say a word, but he didn't need to. Disapproval vibrated from him in angry waves.

"It's all right, Clive," Whit said aloud. "Mother would have liked Mr. Cowrie. She'd *want* him to see her garden. She'd want us to get along with him."

Clive shot a look back and forth between us before reluctantly backing off. He continued to watch me warily as I walked through the gap in the hedge wall.

Of course I must pretend this was my first time seeing the garden, but it wasn't hard to appear awed by the charming little sanctuary. Though the ornamental trees were untrimmed and the beds overgrown and nothing was in bloom, I could imagine how it might have looked at one time, when pruned to perfection. We walked under an arch that supported climbing roses, and I could picture them in abundant bloom. Come spring, there would be white and pink blossoms lacing the trees, and colorful flowers would push their way through the decay of past seasons.

"Pan," I remarked as we passed the mossy, goat-legged god.

Whit nodded. "The god of nature. He played the flute a lot. Mother said he did some not nice things too, but she wouldn't tell any of those stories."

"No, I should think not." I recalled Pan's lecherous nature. Most tales about the god didn't lend themselves to sharing them with children.

"Come here." Whit took my hand and led me, with Clive marching stolidly behind us. I risked a glance back, like Lot's wife, but his grim face didn't turn me to a pillar of salt.

Whit stopped in front of the stone grotto in which the marble statue stood. "Here's where we keep our things."

I looked at the filthy blanket and pillows, the toys and the tin box I'd examined the contents of. "You've got a nice camp here."

Clive watched me from beside the statue.

"Beautiful angel." I rested my fingertips on her white toes. "She looks as if she's watching over you while you play."

"Like Mother," Whit agreed.

"Thank you for sharing this place with me. It's very beautiful, and I can understand why you keep it a secret. When I was a boy, I used to—"

The sound of footsteps crunching on dry leaves turned all our heads. Sir Richard approached, his flapping black coat a stark cutout against the brown-and-gold tones of nature as if a man-sized raven had flown into the garden.

His expression was far more benign than his imposing figure. He smiled in greeting. "I didn't expect to see anyone here. I haven't visited Lavinia's garden in a long time, but today, for some reason, I felt inspired to come."

Something raced past me, Clive hurtling toward his father, planting both hands on Richard's stomach, and shoving against him. "Go!" he screamed.

I blinked in astonishment as the first word I'd ever heard Clive utter was wrenched out of him.

"You don't belong here." Clive pushed again, driving his unresisting father back a few steps. "You killed her!"

Richard appeared as shocked as I felt. He continued to stumble backward when Clive drove all his weight into him. Regaining his composure, he took the boy by the shoulders and held him steady, bending to look his angry son in the eyes. "I didn't, Clive. I swear I didn't. What happened to your mother...wasn't my fault. She took her own life."

I exhaled a pent-up breath. That admission had been hard-won. Richard had grappled with guilt and self blame for many long months, but it seemed he'd finally accepted he truly wasn't responsible for Lavinia's suicide. Now, could Clive do the same?

Father and son remained locked in a silent duel of gazes, while Whitney and I held back, mere observers to their battle.

At last, Clive jerked away from his father's restraining hands. "I *hate* you." He imbued the word with such malevolence, it chilled me. "You didn't protect her. You didn't stop *it*." He spoke as if *it* meant more than her suicide and included the thing that had driven her to the hanging.

Before Richard could reply, Clive ran past him along the path and out of the garden. Richard started after him, then stopped as if uncertain whether to press the issue or allow Clive more time to be angry.

"You tried," I said. "That's a start."

Whit trotted over to stand by his father and touch the sleeve of his coat. "Clive's stubborn. We fight sometimes too, but we always make up in the end."

Richard looked down and grasped Whitney's hand. "I'm sorry I did nothing to prevent her."

Whit didn't answer but pulled his father over to the shrine the boys had set up. He pointed out the dried flowers and colored stones they'd placed around the feet of the statue.

Now Richard stroked the angel's toes with his fingertips. "Your mother would appreciate this tribute. It's lovely." Abruptly, he dropped to a crouch and put his arms around Whitney, drawing him into an embrace that would've melted a colder heart than mine. My eyes stung from the tears, and I quickly wiped them dry and moved away a few paces to give father and son some privacy.

At that moment, I swore I felt a hand against the center of my spine, propelling me forward with a strong push. Richard and Whit looked up as I stumbled toward them.

"I should go after Clive." I gestured in the direction of his retreat.

Richard rose to his full height, and why did that height never cease to thrill me? He held out his hand to shake mine. "Thank you again, for helping me make amends."

My hand slid against his, palm to palm, and I never wanted to let go. "I'm glad if you feel I was of some use."

Richard released first. "I'll see you this afternoon as discussed, and we can address those concerns you have."

I dipped my head in acknowledgment, then hurried away to see if I might find Clive and sort him out. But my heart and most of my mind was back in the garden with Richard and Whit. I wished I could be a part of their reunion, but that wasn't my place. I floated in some nebulous region, something more than an employee, but certainly not family. A facilitator, more than anything.

How I wished I could be more.

CHAPTER 17

I found Clive again, but not until he was ready to be found.

Or I should say, he found us. Whitney and I had already begun eating our lunch when Clive drifted back into the schoolroom. He plunked down in his seat, uncovered his tray, and began to eat. I didn't reprimand him for being tardy. What was the point? Schedules and manners hardly applied to our little group. I addressed him as if he hadn't recently screamed the first words I'd ever heard him speak.

"Have you seen Tom? He's usually the one to deliver lunch, but Molly brought it today."

Clive shrugged. I was torn between wanting to cuff him in the ear and hug him for being the pathetic, melancholy, annoying little arse he was. Why couldn't he have simply accepted his father's apology? But logic and graciousness have never been part of a child's code of conduct, and Richard couldn't expect instant forgiveness after allowing this distance between them to exist for so long.

I discussed our latest chapter of *Robinson Crusoe* with Whit, asking him which part he'd found most exciting. Soon, he and I were mentally on a tropical island, marshalling our meager forces to battle attacking cannibals. If Clive was with us, he gave no sign.

After lunch, I set the boys to doing division problems and turned my attention to my latest story.

"When are you going to tell us what happens next?" Whit asked.

"After it's finished. I'm still figuring things out."

An hour passed during which I wrote little, and then it was time for my appointment with Richard. "Boys, I'll leave you to entertain yourselves. I have something to attend to."

I hurried downstairs, my heartbeats drumming along with my footsteps. I'd tried a number of different beginnings in my mind but still wasn't sure how I was going to broach the subject of a possible supernatural force with Richard. Would he believe my far-fetched tale? And what if he actually did? I wish I came armed with an intelligent course of action to resolve the trouble.

Getting the family moved to their London house, closing up Allinson Hall permanently, and posting signs saying "Death to all who enter here" didn't seem like a viable option. Burning down the place and salting the earth also sounded extreme.

I reached the door of the study and paused to get myself under control before knocking.

"Come in." Richard sat behind his massive desk. *To keep distance between us*, I thought. Smart man.

He gestured me to a chair, and I sat across from him with my hands in my lap. He finished whatever he was writing before regarding me.

"How can I help you, Mr. Cowrie?"

Back to formality again, as if I hadn't witnessed the poignant scene in the garden and received his heartfelt thanks for prompting him to reach out to his sons. The speed with which this man switched between propriety and intimacy made my head spin.

"Well, sir…"

I froze. My hypothesis about a dual haunting seemed utterly ludicrous. I couldn't dare suggest it. *I believe your wife's spirit won't rest until there is accord between you and both your sons. And, by the way, there's a second malevolent entity that haunts your house and thrives on unhappiness. What do you think we should do about it?*

I hesitated for so long, Allinson spoke for me. "If you're still in fear of losing your position, you needn't worry. I'm afraid we're more in need of you than you are of this job." A small smile curved his normally grim mouth.

His assumption of the topic I'd wanted to discuss derailed me. "Ah. I'm pleased to hear that, sir."

He studied me over his interlinked fingers. "I've listened in on your lessons on occasion, and though your teaching methods are unorthodox, to say the least, I believe you are teaching my sons all they need to learn."

"I appreciate your confidence and apologize for the deception I perpetrated."

"Joe Green," he mused. "Why the change in name? A record you wanted to expunge?"

"Nothing quite that dire, sir. It merely seemed too plain and low-class a moniker. I thought Graham Cowrie had a more distinguished ring to it."

He hid his mouth behind those laced fingers, but I saw his smile grow wider.

Now what? I simply couldn't bring myself to tell him my intimations of something evil and dangerous in this house. But I could try to get the family away from its influence. I chose my words carefully.

"I've been considering all you told me about your wife's death and Clive bearing witness to the aftermath. I've wondered if a holiday might be beneficial to you all. Get the boys away from someplace that represents such a grave loss and allow some time for healing. A Mediterranean clime this time of year would not be unwelcome. And after that, return to your London home for the holidays."

Richard sat back in his chair. "I suppose *you* would accompany us on this trip in order to continue the boys' tutelage?"

His rather amused tone annoyed me. For once, I'd offered a suggestion that wasn't self-motivated. I hadn't pictured where I fit into the plan that had only just come to me.

"You mistake my intention. I'm not angling for a free excursion to Italy or Spain. I'm honestly worried about Whitney and, especially, Clive, who seems to grow unhappier by the day. You could also do with some sunshine and relaxation in blue waters."

That small smile curved his lips again. "I do believe you're telling the truth. Your concern for my sons touches me. I will seriously consider your suggestion, although I couldn't take the time until after the holiday season. There are year-end matters here which require my attention. Perhaps later in January."

No. Now. Another few months might be too late. Even another week! I wanted to warn him of my fears, but he'd view me as unhinged. I'd made some progress. Now I could only keep a close eye on Clive and give him little opportunity to go off on his own.

"Is there another matter you wish to discuss?" Richard asked.

Oh, there was plenty, and not all of it to do with the boys or ghosts. I wanted to chat with him about anything other than the doom and gloom of this place. But I shook my head.

"No, sir. I did want to thank you for the loan of books from your library. I enjoyed the Holmes' mysteries immensely and eagerly await further adventures of the detective. Do you know if there are more books planned?"

"I'm not certain. But if you also enjoy mysteries in a lighter vein, I've ordered a collection by Oscar Wilde, *Lord Arthur Savile's Crime and Other Stories*. An amusing diversion, I've been told."

"I would appreciate reading it after you've finished," I said. "And may I recommend to you another Wilde story—a novel which was first serialized in *Lippincott's Monthly* a couple of years ago. *The Picture of Dorian Gray* is terribly sinister and thought provoking. However, for the uncensored version, one must locate back issues of *Lippincott's*. The publishing company saw fit to hack out what they considered objectionable bits before releasing the novel."

Richard's smile grew broader. "I *have* those issues of the original story in its entirety. As a matter of fact, I have a signed copy of installment three."

"By Wilde himself? When did you meet him? May I see?" *Inappropriately informal*, I reminded myself, but I was too excited to care.

"He was present at a party I attended. A very entertaining man with a razor-sharp wit. The periodicals are in the library. I could"—Richard hesitated and frowned—"show the signed copy to you."

I understood his hesitation to tread down this path again. Now we were speaking as fellow reading enthusiasts. And there was something about that library that always seemed to put us on the verge of kissing. His polite invitation felt like an *invitation*, but I knew he didn't want me to misconstrue his meaning.

"I promise to be utterly impressed and jealous that you had the opportunity to meet the great man." I made light of the situation to put Richard at ease.

But as he led the way from his study to the nearby library, I believe we both wondered what might happen next. For attraction always simmered between us. Something invisible yet undeniable tugged us toward each other like a cord of destiny, or an inescapable curse such as that suffered by Dorian Gray.

The library was dim as always, the long brocade drapes closed to keep sunlight from damaging the books. The hushed atmosphere couldn't help but make one feel the need to practically whisper when speaking.

Richard opened a pair of doors at the base of the bookshelf near the fireplace. Inside were stacks of *Lippincott's* and other periodicals. He sorted through them until he found the issues he searched for.

At the library table, we sat side by side to study the magazines in the glow of a lamp. I thumbed through a chapter. "I adore the description of Gray's house and his person. So vivid you can nearly feel yourself there."

Richard pushed another magazine to me, and there was the bold signature of the author himself gracing the end of that month's installment.

"Did Wilde seem as magnetic as the engravings of him in the newspapers? What did he talk about?" I enquired.

"His features are rather too long and prominent to be considered classically handsome, but he's quite striking, with flowing hair and piercing eyes. And when he began to tell a story, even the most self-involved snobs fell silent to listen. He offered satirical, thinly veiled comments at the expense of some of the very people in the room."

I could hardly imagine withdrawn Sir Richard at a glittering society party. But of course, he and his wife must have spent seasons at their London home. They couldn't have always remained secluded in the country. This led me to wonder if Lavinia had been a happier person in town and if her mental state deteriorated at Allinson Hall.

"I've heard it said Wilde lives almost openly with his lover, Lord Alfred Douglas," I gossiped. "Now *there* is a handsome man."

Richard grew stiff, as if the topic struck too close to home. "I couldn't say. I've heard allegations, but know nothing about the man's personal life."

"One would think having money and a presence in society would make it easier to carry on secret affairs. But I sometimes think the lower classes actually have an easier time of it. Fewer eyes watching us and hardly anyone interested in the details of our lives."

Richard remained silent, staring at Wilde's signature. When he spoke again, his voice was so quiet, I understood what an effort it was for him to ask his questions. "How did you carry on with that man you mentioned to me before? How did you carry on your affair?"

"I met Sylvester the way blokes like me often meet gentry coves—in a churchyard. He'd come seeking service, which I provided," I stated baldly. "But it became something more. We talked and laughed afterward, and he sought me out again. And again. Soon he asked if I'd like a nice flat on a quiet street not too far from his house."

"I see." Richard now gazed at his hands, clenched together on the table. "He kept you, then."

"You needn't make it sound so filthy. We were quite happy in the few years we spent together. We each provided what the other needed, companionship and a sexual partner."

"But it didn't last. It couldn't," Richard said almost to himself.

"It could have if Sylvester wanted it to. I would've remained loyal to him for all my days. It was he who lost interest and grazed in greener pastures."

He looked at me at last. "Did he kick you out on the street?"

"Not exactly that rudely, but yes, I had to move to other digs so he could put up his new boy. Luckily, I had an education by then, the skills necessary to find a job with a decent wage." I shook my head. "The loss of a place to live and an allowance didn't matter to me. I cared that the man I placed my faith in no longer cared for me."

Allinson nodded slowly. "That must have hurt terribly. I'm sorry."

I held his gaze. "Will you tell me about yours now? The groom who broke your heart?"

"He didn't… It wasn't like that, and anyway, I don't wish to discuss it."

"I think you do. I believe you'll feel better after sharing the story with one who understands."

He glared at me. "You are rather relentless, aren't you?"

"I've been called so, but I think tenacious sounds more positive. My friends say I've a good ear for listening."

"So I gathered from things you've mentioned about your many friends. But are you any good at keeping the secrets they confide?"

I made a lip-buttoning gesture. "Whatever you tell me in the privacy of this room will not go beyond these walls. You can count on that."

Richard closed the magazine in front of him and sat back in his chair, considering. At last he began to speak. "Jerry Eccleston was a striking man, but I never dreamed of having any sort of dalliance with him. As I said, we started by exercising the horses together. But we'd stop to water them, sit by the stream, and talk. I began to look forward to those daily rides more than anything."

He fell silent for too long, riffling his thumb along the magazine corner. "Though we never did more than talk, the feeling between us grew until it was difficult to ignore."

I knew that desire all too well, since it percolated between us even now.

"We avoided any sign of affection, and at times I thought my desire was one-sided, but when one feels so strongly and sees a certain look in a man's eyes…"

"It's undeniable." I grew suddenly jealous of this Jerry Eccleston, who'd had Richard's first wide-eyed, dewy-fresh love in the palm of his hand and apparently mucked it up.

"One day we could keep apart no longer. What began as an argument, about nothing, really—the condition of the carriage—was an excuse to snarl and butt at each other. And then we collided like two trains."

A tickle of lust pulsed low in my groin. I felt the slow build-up of heat and subsequent explosion he described.

"The fury of our argument carried us from inside the stable to outdoors. In the shade behind the building, we grasped at each other. And then we were suddenly kissing, not caring who might spot us. Such a kiss, I…"

Richard inhaled with a little gasp that made my stomach flip. I craved that sort of a kiss. He'd given me a harsh, bruising one in the chapel, but that was all. Though I'd had this man's cock in my mouth and mine in his, I suddenly wanted much more than that. Cock is cock, but a kiss with the right person could be magical. I pressed my fingers to my lips and waited for the rest of the story.

"No more than that. We simply kissed and held each other, our hands roaming." His eyes were far-seeing, as if he relived the moment again. "When I stepped away, shaking with desire for more, I felt compelled to look up the tower window. Those windows are recessed so deeply, I could hardly see inside, but I detected Lavinia's blue dress, and I knew without a doubt she'd spotted us from her eagle's perch. The exhilaration I'd felt only a second earlier burst like a soap bubble.

"I'd shamed my wife, broken my vows, and destroyed any hope that Lavinia and I could salvage our pitiful marriage."

"All this from one little kiss?" I tried not to sound cheeky but wanted him to understand he continued to judge himself too harshly. "Marriages have survived much worse than the couple leading separate lives and having lovers on the side."

Richard became suddenly aware of me and stared at me as if I'd lost my mind. "She saw me *kissing* a man!"

"Don't you think she'd already guessed at your inclinations?" I asked gently. "Women aren't the innocent fools many husbands think they are. She must have known you had little interest in her sexually and possibly figured out why."

He gave a frustrated click of his tongue. "She was too innocent. She never would have considered it. Lavinia couldn't view what she saw as anything other than a betrayal. I'd begun avoiding her, pretending I didn't know she spent most of her days up in that damned tower while I was out riding the countryside. Though I sent Jerry away that very day, it was too late. Lavinia hanged herself that same night."

"You *fired* the bloke? On the spot? No second chances? You just cut him loose?" So much for my assumption Eccleston was a heartbreaker. Allinson had behaved like Leighton, taking what he wanted from a man and then chucking him out.

Richard frowned. "I gave him a stellar reference, but I had to send Jerry away to prove to her I wouldn't stray again. You're missing the point. Lavinia was so distraught, she *killed* herself because of what she witnessed."

"Many things lead a person to give up hope in life. That transgression was probably the least of what troubled her."

The moment was tailor-made for me to bring up my theory of an evil entity with the capability to twist a person's mind and fill her with enough sadness to make her seek solace in death. But I still couldn't bring myself to voice the outlandish proposition to Richard, especially not when he was already glaring at me.

"I thought you'd realized her death wasn't your fault. That's what you told the boys," I reminded him. "So will you continue to let guilt eat you away from the inside, or will you offer yourself a pardon and a fresh start?"

He rubbed the heels of his hands into his eyes, shoulders slumped in exhaustion. "I've mucked things up so badly on all fronts, I don't know if I can ever fully forgive myself."

"A little bit, then." I put my thumb and forefinger an inch apart. "You've done well by repairing things with Whitney, and you can keep trying with Clive. You must let go of your guilt about Lavinia. As for Jerry Eccleston, you might find out where the man landed and send him a note of apology."

He drew his hands away from his eyes and looked at me. "I did treat him rather shabbily. That hardly occurred to me, given everything else I've done wrong. Thank you for reminding me of yet another reason to feel guilty."

I smiled. "That's your fatal flaw. You need to stop thinking that way. Look at me. I've misbehaved many times in my life but never feel guilty. It's a debilitating emotion that does no one any good."

"You are very wise for a man with no code of ethics." He almost smiled back.

"I have ethics, but they're my own brand." I gave him a wink.

Richard snorted, then burst into laughter, which naturally made me laugh too. And soon we were uncontrollably chuckling about a joke that wasn't all that clever. My amusement wound down, but Richard laughed until he gasped for breath and tears rolled down his cheeks, a release he'd sorely needed.

"See how much better you feel?" I rested my hand on his sleeve and squeezed the hard arm underneath. Richard turned his palm up, and I slid mine down his sleeve to clasp his hand, our fingers entwined. He wiped his eyes with his free hand and looked at me.

Stripped bare of his aloof manner and arrogant bearing, Richard was simply a beautiful, vulnerable wreck of a man, yearning for affection. Affection I was happy to give.

CHAPTER 18

I leaned closer, paused, and moved again until my mouth hovered a breath away from his. He didn't draw back but bent toward me. I seized the kiss from his lips with a delicate pluck, his soft, warm mouth opening sweetly under mine. I took a taste of it…and another…each kiss deeper until at last my tongue swept inside and rolled over his. Our lips mashed together with bruising force. Ah, this was the kiss I'd wanted, a passionate merging that echoed through me like a gong.

Our hands were still awkwardly clasped on the table. I let go to cup his face. The scrape of stubble against my palm made me shiver. I wished I could feel that scrape on my inner thighs. Cradling the hard contour of his jaw, I rubbed a thumb idly at the corner of his mouth, then pulled back to study the mouth I'd been feasting on. The damp, plump lower lip begged to be bitten. I traced its curve, and when Richard's lips parted, I slipped my finger inside. His tongue bumped against it, teeth nibbling lightly.

At the gentle pressure of my finger, his mouth opened, jaw dropping slightly. I gazed at that open mouth, and my cock ached to fill it. I envisioned pushing Richard onto his knees and standing in front of him, feeding my staff to him. Soon, but not yet.

I kissed him again, wide, wet, seductive kisses I bet his burly groom hadn't known how to deliver. I was determined to out-kiss a man I'd never met, to make Richard forget Eccleston had ever existed, to become the *only* lover to occupy his thoughts and his body. The feeling of jealousy didn't suit me. I hadn't been this put out even the day I'd met Sylvester Leighton on the street with his new lover by his side.

My feelings might have been hurt by Sylvester's abandonment, but I understood the ways of the world and hadn't been shocked or too emotionally devastated by his shift of affections. This unexpected rush of unadulterated annoyance at Eccleston and possessiveness of Richard, a man I'd never own, took me aback. My normally even keel seemed to be disrupted by choppy waves.

Sitting in side-by-side chairs while attempting to get closer was impossible. I shoved mine aside and sat on the library table to face Richard. He stood and moved between my legs, his hands at my waist. I locked my legs behind him, pulling him nearer, tangling my fingers in his hair and holding his head so I could kiss him more fiercely. *Snug as two bugs in a rug*, as my mum used to say. The heat between our bodies built to an unbearable level. Barriers of constricting clothing needed to be shed.

For prolonged moments, we remained lost to the world around us. Nothing existed but the union of our mouths, the press of two bodies together, my erection rubbing against his hardness. The mounting pleasure in my cock made me fear I'd spill in my smalls like an undisciplined youth. What an ignoble conclusion that would be. But young and uncontrolled was rather how I felt with Richard, as green and fresh as if I hadn't had sex many times in my life.

Suddenly, his large hands weren't gripping my waist but pushing me away. His mouth broke from mine and he gasped, "No."

I nearly whimpered. More self-denial and recrimination and why? I wanted to slap some sense into the man. Or perhaps get him drunk enough to act as uninhibited as he'd been that night in the chapel.

THE TUTOR

I gazed into his eyes, so close I could see the difference between black pupils and deep-brown irises. He was flushed and breathing erratically.

"No. Not *here*." Richard stepped back, took my hand, and pulled me off the library table. "Over in the corner, we'll be more hidden."

Yes, indeed, sir. Take me where and how you like. I'm ready.

I happily followed him to the dimmest corner of the room, a sheltered nook between a wall of books and a standing bookcase. We'd be out of sight if a servant entered the room, although it seemed no one ever cleaned here.

As I removed layers of Richard's clothing and he tore away mine, I wondered if Lavinia would chuck another book at my head. But if her spirit was present, she apparently didn't mind the things we did. Maybe she enjoyed watching, the little minx. I chuckled at the thought.

"What?" Richard murmured against my chest where he tongue-bathed my nipple.

"Nothing. Just some foolishness." I stroked his hair and gave a hiss as he bit my nipple. "Thinking how it would feel to lie naked on the library table with you fucking me. Smithers would bring in a tea tray and pretend he saw nothing."

"Don't." He nipped the other erect nub, and a flash of pleasure/pain shot through me. "There's no humor in getting caught."

"Oh, sir, there's humor in *everything* if one only looks for it."

After that, I was finished talking. There were better things to do with my mouth such as more kissing, licking the hard planes of Richard's mostly nude body, and at last, dropping to my knees to suck him. The satisfying heft and girth of his cock filled my hand. I licked the length teasingly while looking up at him. No liquor-glazed eyes this time. He was fully present and staring down at me with a heat that might incinerate me.

Every long stroke of my tongue or nibble with my teeth and the hard suction when I fully enveloped him made my own cock feel those things. I'd been on the receiving end before, so I knew exactly how that pleasure felt to him. Each contented groan or grimace of pleasure Richard gave became mine. Thus my tension mounted along with his.

When he came, it happened abruptly. His body went rigid, and he leaned back into the wall of books, gripping shelves on either side. A spasm of cock and a burst of semen in my throat, and his climax was over. I let go and climbed to my feet, took Richard's hot muscular body in my arms, and held him. I inhaled warm flesh and snaked out my tongue to taste salt. My full erection nestled snugly against his belly, and I was completely content—or close enough to it.

Richard came back to himself with a shuddering breath. He slid a hand between us to cup my length. "So very hard," he marveled.

"For you. I've dreamed of this moment for days."

He gave my balls a little squeeze. "You knew this was bound to happen again."

"Of course I knew. I banked on it. 'Twas like holding back the tide…impossible." I smiled into the soft hollow between his collarbones and placed a kiss there.

"Let me return the favor, then." He let go of me and began to lower himself. There was nothing I craved more than the sight of Sir Richard Allinson kneeling at my feet, but just then I wanted him in my embrace even more. An odd and unexpected feeling.

"That's all right." I urged him to stand. "Hold me now and bring me off with your hand. Then, after you're ready again, we can do something new."

For the next bit, I thought of nothing concerning spirits, hauntings, or death, and it was lovely. I turned around in the circle of his arms so we stood with my back to his front. I leaned my head against his shoulder and watched him grip my rigid cock and stroke it. The sight of his large fist surrounding me was a pleasure all on its own.

As he applied greater pressure and moved his fist more briskly, I writhed against him. His breath bathed my cheek, and he sheltered my body with his. The sensation of his strength supporting me was bliss itself. I half closed my eyes and moaned. The final element to perfect the moment would be a full-length mirror standing in front of us.

I imagined how we'd appear together: a large man and slighter one, half-naked and entwined together, Richard's handsome face in profile as he bent his head to bite my shoulder, my mouth open in ecstasy, his hand moving capably now on my cock as if it were his own. At that moment, it *was* his.

I let my body melt into his, felt his erection returning, pressing against my rear. I sagged into him and trusted he'd keep me upright. The relentless beat of lust throbbing in my cock and balls grew faster and faster until it reached an unbearable pitch. If that feeling were audible, it would be a high-pitched whistle only dogs could hear. And then…

I cried out and erupted, jets of white shooting as if from a pistol to spatter the spines of several books on the shelf facing me. I shook and gulped air, and after I opened my eyes, stared at ejaculate dripping down a dark-green book cover. Joy, ecstasy, and hilarity erupted from my mouth as come had exploded from my cock. I laughed, and a lightness of being filled me. There was no room for any negative feelings. I was exactly where I wanted to be, and life couldn't be more perfect.

Behind me, Richard gave a low rumble of laughter too. He kissed my neck, my shoulder, sucked on my earlobe. "You looked so…"

"I felt so…" I replied. "And now, if you're ready, I'd like to feel more."

Where was a library table to be bent over when I needed one? I slipped out of Richard's arms and faced the wall of books. I gripped a shelf low enough that I had to bend over, arse thrusting invitingly upward. Richard needed no prompting to move behind me and guide his erection to my entrance. The tip of his probing cock made my body clench eagerly. I couldn't wait to feel the familiar stretching sensation when he filled me.

But he paused with his hands on my hips. "Are you…quite ready? Like this with no, er…preparation?"

"Wet your cock. Slick it well, and it will slide in."

Naturally, it would be better with some oily substance, but one made do when lubricants weren't at hand.

I glanced over my shoulder. "Don't be a namby-pamby gentleman. Work up some spit. And don't look so worried. You won't get hurt."

"I fear I'll hurt *you*. It doesn't seem possible to fit into…" Again he trailed off.

"You'd be surprised how the body accommodates." I faced forward again, braced my legs more, took a firmer grip on the shelf, and waited. Seconds later, a thick cockhead pushed past the outer ring of muscle.

"So tight," Richard breathed. Still, he kept pushing.

I relaxed into the stretching, almost burning sensation. The pressure was intense at first, then less so as my body adjusted. Mild discomfort turned to exhilarating sensation as he filled my channel more deeply. Richard's legs bumped against mine, his groin against my arse, his member buried to the hilt in me. We were joined as tightly as could be, for when I nudged my rear back toward him, he could enter no farther.

"Oh, good Christ," he muttered and curved his body over mine, belly to my back, his hands gripping several shelves above mine. Again I pictured how we looked, the perfect curve of our two bodies together as they became one.

Richard withdrew slowly. My body reluctantly released him, but not for long. Another thrust, and he was part of me again. I stared at the floor, wooden boards warped with age and creaking with our every movement. Richard impaled me with a strong thrust, and I grunted at the impact. It hurt and felt amazing, and I needed more. His skin slid over mine, friction building between us as he began to pump faster.

My gaze shifted from the floor to the shelf in front of me, passing over a blue book with a long title in French. I idly wondered what it said, and I immediately lost interest as Richard gave another powerful thrust.

He paused and pressed a kiss between my shoulder blades. "All right? I'm not going too deep?"

"Fine," I assured him. "Deep is good. There's a place inside like a spot on a treasure map. When you strike it, the feeling is intense. Truth be told, I don't mind some roughness. Bang away."

That rarely-heard-but-so-delicious chuckle flowed over me like melted butter. And then Sir Richard began to fuck me with a focused intensity that stole my breath and set that old floor creaking until I thought we'd break through it. I clung hard to the shelf, fingers cramping. My body swayed against the onslaught. But, oh yes, that power was *exactly* what I craved. I gritted my teeth and rode the pain and exhilaration.

I wondered what this was like for Richard, his first time with a man. How did it compare to lying with his wife? Proper ladies were taught to lie very still and pretend sex wasn't happening. Was this sensation tighter, harder, more driven and passionate? Was sex with a man everything Richard had dreamed it would be when he'd imagined such things? Did he think of the groom he'd fallen in love with and wish I was that man?

He'll never mistake me for some other bloke. I won't let him, I decided.

I tried to straighten, pushing back against Richard. After one or two more strokes, he pulled out. "I'm sorry. What have I done?"

I turned to him with a smile. "Nothing. But I wish to see you when you come."

His handsome face was flushed, sweat shining on his brow. He blinked. "It can be done facing each other? Even with a man?"

Oh, my sweet innocent. Give me time, and I'll show you all sorts of positions you never guessed at. "Yes. It can be done face-to-face. Only a little maneuvering is required."

I rested a foot on one of the shelves of the bookcase and beckoned Richard close. Putting my hands on his shoulders, I tilted my pelvis forward, better presenting my rear.

Richard needed no encouragement to try this new angle and barely had to guide his tip to me. His cock already knew the way to where it wanted to be. One long slow push, and he was back inside me. My cock, full-staff once more, brushed against his stomach as he moved. My grip on his shoulders held me steady, and his hands on my arse kept me firmly in place. I angled my body even more to give him full access, and I looked into his face, studying the myriad expressions that flitted across his features.

When I first met Richard, his eyes had seemed windows to a dark, doomed soul. Now I saw light there, joy and hope and the possibility of happiness. I believed *I* had helped turn on that light, brought him out of gloom and back into the world, and I felt fairly smug about that.

I pressed my body as close as I was able as he thrust into me. Richard's expression shifted from grim determination through mounting pleasure to the dawning of bliss. His transformation was glorious, the moment of his climax a revelation. I held tight while he trembled in my arms, and when he'd finished, I continued to embrace him, reluctant to let go.

For several moments, we remained breathing in unison, hearts madly thumping together. The floor creaked under our weight, and the clock on the fireplace mantel ticked, small, comforting sounds that made this place feel like an impenetrable bubble.

But, as unlikely as a servant breaching our bookish fortress was, we'd lingered, nearly naked, for long enough. We pulled apart to hastily dress. I wondered if Richard would offer me another kiss before we went our separate ways.

As he straightened his tie and smoothed his waistcoat, he regarded me. "Thank you for that. I didn't mean to ever…"

"I know."

"You're rather irresistible." A smile wafted across his lips, reddened from the pressure of our kisses. "But I don't want to take advantage of you, a man in my employ."

I fastened my fly. "No advantage was taken. I believe what two people consent to in private is no one's business but their own."

"I wish all of society held such an enlightened view. You are a revelation, Graham Cowrie." He reached out a hand and lightly touched my face, cupped my jaw, and leaned in. The pressure of his lips was fleeting but set off an earthquake inside me. That simple peck was sweeter than the passionate fury of all our earlier ones, and left me shaken.

"I must return to my work now," Richard murmured.

"And I to the boys."

Butut we remained a little longer, locked in a silent moment in which it seemed volumes were spoken, although neither of us said a word.

CHAPTER 19

My mum had another saying she was fond of bandying about on the rare occasions when things went well for us. "It's only a matter of time. This world isn't made of sunshine, and a cloudy day is coming soon."

Amazing I kept my generally positive attitude after living with such a pessimist. Her words became a self-fulfilling prophecy as Mum herself brought sadness and ruin into our house in the form of Roger Dwyer.

Over the next few weeks, it seemed grace had befallen me in Allinson Hall. All the haunting presences withdrew to their proper place—a dim memory. I awoke from no more nightmares of choking to death or running relentlessly to escape an unseen attacker. Nor did I have any messages or signs of Lavinia's spirit prompting me to save her family. It was easy to put aside my worries and feel I'd overdramatized the whole thing.

When Whitney brought me two bundles of fragrant herbs tied to primitive figures made of braided hay and said he'd found them under his and Clive's beds, I knew Tom had crafted them. The wards seemed foolishly superstitious in my new frame of mind.

"I believe Tom is trying to protect you boys from nightmares," I told Whit. "A kind gesture that does no harm. Why don't you leave them where you found them?"

My fears for the twins' safety receded. Everything seemed to be going well, and I was distracted by new romance, viewing everything through a hazy glow. Yes, the brothers still seemed to be at odds, but they'd get past their quarrel eventually. Yes, Clive hardly spoke, but now he communicated a little, so I chose to see that as an improvement. He was no quieter, more withdrawn, or prone to disappearing for stretches of time than he ever had been before, I told myself. And I was happy to believe that fiction.

I was too focused on my dream come true, almost nightly visits with Richard. In the late hours, we'd meet in the chapel or library, or I'd slip into his grand bedroom and his massive bed, never my own room, which was too near the boys.

We spent time together—not only fucking, although that required a considerable amount of our attention, but talking, eating, drinking, and making silly jokes together. I learned the dour man had a sense of humor after all and glimpsed the boy he'd once been, the man he could still be if he sloughed off the burden of this house and of fighting his desires. Over several weeks, we became lovers in every sense of the word, and all dark thoughts evaporated.

Sir Richard continued to come around the schoolroom several times a week, and sometimes, on fine days we'd meet him outdoors. Once he even participated in a game of tag, chasing a laughing Whit around a circular garden bed until both of them collapsed breathless in dead leaves. I was so entranced by the sight of father and son finding joy in each another's company that I felt more annoyed than sympathetic toward Clive, who remained distant and scowling like a disapproving gargoyle.

I walked over to him. "Why don't you join in? This stubbornness has gone on long enough. Will you cling to blame for the rest of your life?"

Clive shot me a look the equivalent of pouring boiling oil on invaders then marched off toward the house and disappeared inside.

I could have gone after him. I could've insisted he remain outdoors with us, or at least spent time alone with him, trying to bridge the chasm. I didn't do either of those things. I simply let him go.

Just then, Richard rose and turned his attention to catching me, since he hadn't succeeded with Whit. I was happy to run away and led him a merry chase all the way into the hidden garden. The moment we were out of sight of the house or Whit or any watching eyes, I let him catch and kiss me until I had to cling to his shoulders to remain upright.

I hadn't been this happy or content since the heady days when Leighton first pulled me up from the mud pit of Spitalfields, washed me off, dressed me up, and started me on my road to becoming a new man.

But this was even better, I realized one night as I lay beside Richard's furnace of a body, breathing slowly and deeply as he slept. I was even more joy filled because I—knowledge struck me and a bolt of fear along with it. Because I *loved* Richard Allinson.

And his sons.

And the sense of having something almost like a family, which I hadn't experienced since I was very young.

Love was an almost unknown quantity to me. I'd held deep affection and gratitude toward dear Sylvester, and very much liked other lovers over the years, but this voracious, all-consuming desire for a man was something quite new. The more hours I spent with Richard, the deeper grew my yearning to have even more time together. A relationship, doomed to be short-lived, had become far too important to me. I'd never expected that development.

This world isn't made of sunshine, and a cloudy day is coming soon. Mother's words rang in my head in that crystalline moment when I realized I'd fallen in love. But I was able to pretend her warning wasn't true—for a time.

One very late night, Richard and I were again stretched across the small country of his ridiculously oversized bed, reading in companionable silence. We lay in opposite directions; I stretched on my stomach with my book propped before me, Richard sitting upright, several pillows supporting his back.

I'd nearly reached the thrilling moment in the story when the detective would unveil the perpetrator of the crime and explain how the deed was done. I read faster, heart pounding with anticipation to see if my guess was correct.

A fingertip traced a tickling line from my heel to my toes over the arch of my foot, pulling me back from the brink. I glanced at my lover over one shoulder. "You are an annoying man."

"You shouldn't have your feet near my face."

"Do they reek?" I demanded, shoving my toes closer.

He growled and grabbed my foot, and I was made to pay horribly for my impertinence as he tickled me mercilessly. I twisted my body with my ankle still in his grip and pushed at his arm with my free foot. He ignored it and continued to tickle until I was breathless with laughter and squirming to get away. Both our books went crashing to the floor, and pillows went flying off the bed in the ensuing struggle.

I broke loose long enough to nearly crawl away. He caught me and dragged me back onto the mattress, pinning me under his great weight until I called a muffled "I surrender" into the bedding.

I turned my face and gasped, "Get off me, you great oaf."

Richard chuckled and rolled aside to lie beside me. I nipped the large biceps so near my mouth, then kissed the spot I'd bitten. "I enjoy your company too much."

"And I yours." He looked sideways at me. "Far too much. I spend most of my days dreaming of the upcoming night. It can make it difficult to concentrate on my duties."

"What duties does a gentleman *have*, exactly?" I teased. "Isn't it simply to dress nicely and be seen at social events? That's what I learned in London."

"Some gentlemen get by with little more than making the social rounds and spending a lot of time at their clubs. But those who take their responsibilities seriously tend to a hundred little details about the various properties and tenants. I confer with my land agent about the crops being raised and chances for improved yield with alternate crops or better seed. I hear the tenants' grievances and try to alleviate their concerns as much as possible."

"All that? To hear tell at the pub, you're practically a stranger in their midst. I can't imagine anyone bringing any complaints to your doorstep."

"I learn these things through my agent. I don't actually stop in at the cottages." A small frown furrowed his brow, and I considered maybe it was time to stop joking. Richard clearly took his position in the community to heart.

"They respect you," I hastened to add. "They just don't know you as I do. You're some mythic, mysterious figure to them."

Richard tapped a finger on his bare chest. "My grandfather was quite a popular landlord. He won both the admiration and respect of the locals. He recalled everyone's name down to the tiniest newborn. But when my father inherited, he lost the store of goodwill Grandfather had built."

"What did your father do?"

"Nothing. That was the problem. He spent most of his time in London—with his mistress, I learned later. Mother was bitter, disappointed in her life here, and made no effort in the community. When it was my turn to take the reins, I vowed I'd drive the estate better than my parents had.

Fiscally, I've brought it back from the brink, but I've never had the knack of being personable. Still, I've kept the land intact, and I suppose that's the important thing."

I thought of how the men in the village had spoken of Allinson as cold and distant and wished every one of them could know how much he cared for their community, even if he didn't know how to behave in an affable way. I felt greatly privileged to have been allowed to see his other side, the warm, laughing fellow who tickled my feet and made love with the intensity of a diamond-tipped cutting blade.

"Go around the pub once in a while," I suggested. "Share a pint. Let the commoners know you as more than lord of the manor."

The finger on his chest tapped faster. "I wouldn't know what to say."

"You're a shy chap at heart. That's your secret. If you don't know what to talk about, ask them about their lives. Those men will go on for hours with very little prompting."

"I should tell you something." Richard abruptly changed the subject. "I've thought about what you said concerning removing the boys from the house where their mother died. There are too many sad memories for them here, especially Clive."

My drowsy, sated, post-sex mood evaporated, and I was instantly wide awake. "So you plan to move to the London house for a while?"

I would be able to see my old friends again in my free time. The idea was exhilarating. There might be difficulty in finding ways to be alone with Richard in the smaller city house with staff all around, but we'd manage to carry on. Perhaps sometimes we'd take the boys to the art gallery or zoological gardens. Or the museum. They'd love the Egyptian display. Away from this house, Clive would likely improve so I could stop worrying about whether I should be doing more to protect him from that evil influence.

"How soon are you planning the move?" I asked.

"You misunderstand me." Now, all four of Richard's fingers drummed quickly. "I've concluded it's past time the boys went to school. I myself was sent at age eight. I thought keeping them home would give them time to grieve for their mother. They'd been through enough upheaval without facing the daunting move into a dormitory. But now I believe it would be healthier for them to be around lads their own age and follow the normal course of a boy's education. I've made special arrangements to have them enrolled mid school year. Next term, in fact."

I felt as if I'd been slapped across the face by one of those Eton teachers Leighton had told me horror stories of. From everything Sylvester had said, a proper British gentleman's education was near to criminal neglect of the spirit. There was no room for a dreamy or nonathletic lad, no quarter given to the artistic or inquisitive soul, no kindness or nurturing for a boy who was a little different. Leighton claimed his years in boarding school were hell on earth.

Besides, with no more need for a tutor for the boys, I'd be booted out the door. The casual way Richard had informed me of the news suggested he didn't care that our time together would be coming to an end. Maybe he'd never seen me as more than a body to ease his needs and warm his bed for a while. Something less than a person and easily cut loose—just as he'd fired Eccleston when he became inconvenient. Just as Leighton had abandoned me when he grew bored and wanted something new.

I'd made the mistake of forgetting I was expendable, the error of beginning to feel things I shouldn't have felt.

"So, you've decided that, have you?" I felt suddenly far too vulnerable lying on my back, naked. I climbed off the big bed and began to hunt for my clothes.

"I believe it's best for the boys, don't you?"

I didn't dare turn to look at him lest he see the emotions I barely controlled. "I'm certain it would be better for them to be away from here." I scooped my smalls from the floor and thrust a leg in.

"It was inevitable they'd leave for school." He sounded almost as if he were pleading with me.

"Of course it was." I found my trousers half underneath the bed along with Richard's open book facedown on the floor. I closed the book and set it on the nightstand, then put on my trousers.

"I would compensate you for lost wages for the next several months."

The offer felt like a knife between my shoulder blades. But hadn't I come here for the money? I'd be paid and have plenty of opportunity to search for a better position.

"Naturally I'd give you an impeccable reference," Richard continued.

"Very generous, considering what you learned about my credentials. I couldn't be more grateful." It was all I could do to offer the clipped words of appreciation.

"There are still several weeks before the boys would leave. In the meantime, I'll require help preparing them for the move, acquiring uniforms, packing everything and the like. There's no need for you to leave for quite some time."

"I serve at your command," I gritted through clenched teeth. *I won't cry. I will* not *burst into tears like a schoolgirl with crushed hopes and dashed dreams.*

The bed creaked, and soft footsteps padded up behind me. His hand rested heavily on my shoulder, and I winced from the pain of that touch.

"I didn't know how to tell you," he murmured. "I shall miss your presence greatly. If I could think of any way, some way that we could manage to…"

Even now, that low, hoarse voice sent my belly into a slow, lazy roll and rubbed my flesh like warm velvet. How could he affect me so when all I wanted to do was turn and slap him hard enough to sting my palm?

"I shall miss you too, but time moves on," I said so lightly the words nearly bumped against the ceiling.

I moved away from his hand on my shoulder, found my undershirt, and put it on. "It's not as if I expected any other outcome. So au revoir to you and your darling sons. I'm certain they'll take to school like ducks to water. Especially Clive. He won't have any difficulties at all fitting in."

"There's no call for sarcasm. It was your suggestion I remove the boys from Allinson Hall. What did you expect me to do with them? Boys go to boarding school. It's what's done." Confused and bemused, his tone did nothing to allay my rising fury.

"I expect you to show some empathy toward them, especially Clive, who witnessed something so gruesome, something no child should ever have to see, and then had to pretend as if he didn't see it."

Now I did turn to face him, for I was armed with anger that masked everything else. "I expect you to give them time to heal in a more pleasant environment than this one—your London house. Exiling them to survive amongst the savage brutes who rule at a boys' school is…" I shook my head, unable to come up with words strong enough. "I expected better of you."

He glared back at me. "What do you know of it, *Joe Green*? You never went to school or lived among those brutes, as you call them."

I slipped into the thickest East End accent I could muster. "No, guv'nor. I'm talking above me place. A bloke like me knows nuffin' of bullies with hard hands and sneering words. I'm sure it's all peaches 'n' cream at a toff school and wish I'd been blessed to go to one instead of bein' the ignorant bugger boy I am."

Richard clicked his tongue and turned away. "I can't talk with you when you act this way. You're disappointed. I understand. We'll speak again later after you've calmed down."

After I've calmed down? After I've fucking calmed down? Rage thundered through me at his dismissive tone. I was inches away from launching myself at him, letting my weight and gravity drive his body to the floor, pummeling until he begged me to stop. Of course it wouldn't turn out that way. He'd have me flipped and pinned in a heartbeat, and then I'd have no shred of pride left as he straddled me and watched tears trickle down my cheeks.

But I could do one thing with grace—make an exit. I put on my shirt, gathered my socks and shoes, and stalked out of the room without saying good-bye.

And then I continued to stalk, metaphorically speaking. I went to my room and began jamming everything I owned into my valise and trunk. It was the dead of night. There would be no carriage to take me to the train depot, but fiery anger would serve to fuel my long walk to the village. I'd catch the first train to London tomorrow and send for my trunk later—or just leave everything behind. I'd started from scratch before. I could do it again.

It tore out my heart to think of leaving the boys without explanation, but I couldn't linger while my powerful thrust of anger fizzled and turned into something weak and whimpering. I penned a note each for Whit and Clive and left them on the school table, along with the mystery story I'd nearly finished, scribbling an explanation of who the culprit had been. They might read the story, if they cared to.

Was it cowardly for me to sneak away in the night? Probably. Had I done worse things in my life? Certainly. The boys might be a little upset for a while, but they'd soon forget the brief time when I'd been their teacher. Likely they'd put me out of mind sooner than I would them as other things rose to all-consuming importance in their young lives. What was I to them, after all? Merely their tutor.

CHAPTER 20

My feet were sore and my arm ached from carrying the heavy valise by the time I finally reached the village. But it was well past dawn, so at least the shops were starting to open. I bought a newly made roll from the baker's wife and sat on the low stone wall of the village green to feast on hot, fresh bread. The yeasty goodness filled my stomach and eased my inner turmoil a little.

The long walk had served to dissipate my fury, which, as expected, turned into whimpering sadness and aching disappointment. I couldn't change what was going to happen. Richard would send his boys to school when he saw fit, and I would move on to some other post. It was foolish to leave without pay or a reference simply because my pride had been hurt. I should go back. I'd prepare the boys for school not only physically but mentally, warning them what to expect, giving them tips on how to survive bullying. I'd be a general sending his soldiers into battle. What a stupid waste of energy this walk had been, for now I had to go all the way back. If I was lucky, no one would even notice I'd been away.

Sitting on that cold stone wall watching the sun rise and the village awaken, I continued wavering between facing up to my responsibility to the boys or fleeing, as free as one of those swallows swooping past. My decision began to drift the other way. I didn't *have* to put my tail between my legs and slink back to Allinson Hall. I had enough money in my pocket to buy a train ticket for London, where I could reinvent myself again and find new work or maybe even beg my way back into that typesetting job. I never had to face Richard Allinson and his melting eyes again. I never had to feel his hands on my flesh, his cock pumping into my body, his…

"Grrr." My growl of annoyance caused a dog sniffing nearby to shy away and cast me a wounded look as if I'd kicked it. I tossed the shaggy beast the last crust of my bread and hopped off the wall.

The mercantile store where the post office counter was located had opened. I decided to check for any mail that may have arrived for me and hadn't yet been delivered to the Hall. I wasn't ready to begin my long walk back *or* go to the train depot to check on the train schedule.

Mrs. Gorman, the shopkeeper, gave me a wide smile from the shelves where she unpacked a box of threads and buttons. "Mr. Cowrie, what in the world brings you to town at this hour of the morning?"

"I woke so very early, I thought I might as well get a start on enjoying my day off. It was a brisk walk, though."

"I imagine. Up before the dawn with the wind as cutting as it is today, you could catch your death. Mark my words, there'll be icy rain and maybe even a little snow before the day is through. You should make your purchases and head for shelter before the weather hits."

"I'll be sure to. Do you have any letters for me, Mrs. Gorman?"

"I believe I do." She bustled into a back room and emerged with a handful of posts. "If you would deliver these to the Hall, it would save Percy the trip out."

"Certainly." I took the mail and put it in my coat pocket. I'd left my valise outside the door, not wanting to have to explain its existence to nosy Mrs. Gorman. I bid her good-bye and went to retrieve the bag and walk to the pub for a pint while I read my correspondence.

"First customer of the day," the barkeep greeted me. "Early for ale."

"Never too early, Mr. Stump." I took a seat at the table that had already become mine after only a few visits to the place and read my letter while I waited for the pub owner to pour me a glass.

My name in Madame Alijeva's spidery handwriting flowed beautifully across the envelope. Inside were three well-filled pages strongly scented with rosewater.

My darling boy, the note began. In a few lines, and in English that was much better in writing than filtered through her thick accent, Madame filled me in on current events in her life and those of a couple of mutual friends. Then she got to the meat and potatoes of the haunting I'd told her about.

I agree, the experiences you describe suggest more than one energy. One is likely the deceased Mrs. Allinson seeking only the happiness of her loved ones. The other may be a very dark spirit indeed, perhaps even a demon spawned from Hell itself.

The woman certainly did have a flare for the dramatic. That was why she held her customers' belief in the palm of her hand.

Have you a rosary? No, of course you would not, heathen boy. I recommend you get one and some holy water. Sprinkle it around your bed at night to keep the evil spirit away as you sleep.

Where did she think I was? There was no Catholic church in this part of the country from which I could steal holy water.

Such rare manifestations are insidious, pure evil, and may be difficult to cast out. They sometimes reveal themselves as a black mist but often are no more than a feeling of dread or despair. Their desire is to possess and control living persons' spirits.

Yes, I'd figured all that out already. Now if she'd only get to the part about how to eradicate them.

Your best course of action would be to leave the haunted dwelling, but if that is not possible, you may take precautions to protect yourself and those who seem most tormented by the entity.

That would be Clive. It suddenly occurred to me why I no longer suffered from those awful, hopeless feelings. The thing in the tower had turned its attention from me to Clive. How had I not realized that before? *Because you were too caught up in playing games with Richard.*

The barman approached from behind and plunked a glass down on the table. His unexpected move made the pages rattle in my hand.

"Steady on. You're in a state this morning. Fight with a lady last night? Cast you out, did she?"

"Something like that," I muttered and resumed reading.

Burning sage to cleanse the air of evil is one easy remedy. Prayer and religious icons, a crucifix or picture of Christ placed at the site you believe is the source from which the entity emanates.

I hadn't noticed so much as one religious-themed painting in the entire house. But there was that cross on the chapel altar. It was solid stone and would be like hauling Christ's actual cross up Golgotha to carry it to the top of the tower. Still, I had pitifully little to work with, and I did want to quell that evil energy before I left Allinson Hall. Even though the boys would be gone, they'd come home on holidays, and meanwhile, the thing might find someone else to torment. Timid little Molly, perhaps? Or Richard! A picture of him in the depths of despair, deciding to end it all, pistol in hand, flashed in my mind.

You must understand these evil spirits play a game with mortals. They may remain inactive for years, bothering no one, then, when there are strong emotions to feed upon and the right vessel, they attack. It is likely this creature slowly drove the poor lady of the house to hang herself. Those already saddened by life are an easier target. Perhaps this evil entity holds sway over her ghostly spirit even now, keeping her its prisoner in eternity.

Besides affecting moods, such entities may even become powerful enough to move or throw objects or create strong winds. These energies are not to be taken lightly simply because they cannot be seen.

Back to methods of how to get rid of it, please, Madame. I read on...

I know you are a nonbeliever, which will make trust in any religious icon seem foolish, but it is not *the cross itself that holds power. It is the faith. Faith in a higher power. Faith in goodness. Faith in love. Only light may dispel darkness. Good luck, my darling.* I could almost hear the strong roll of the *r* and her thick and juicy *els*. *I hope to see you in springtime in the city where you belong.*

Thanks for nothing! She'd given me little new information on dispelling a demon. Just a lot of religious twaddle. Perhaps the best I could do would be to get the boys out of the house as soon as possible. Maybe suggest a shopping trip in London before school.

Whatever I was going to do, I knew now it didn't include taking the next train out of town. I wouldn't abandon the boys or their father. Not as long as I still might be of use to them. Score one for Lavinia, who'd made me her champion in the fight against Evil with a capital E.

I finished my ale, left a few coins on the table for the barman, picked up my valise, and began the long trudge back to Allinson Hall.

CHAPTER 21

As Mrs. Gorman predicted, the weather grew worse with every minute that passed. I marched straight into a cold wind that pierced all layers of clothing and chilled me to the skin. Grit peppered my face, and soon a smattering of raindrops joined the dirt bombarding me. I could no longer feel my feet as they plodded forward, and my hands were icy since I'd accidentally left my gloves at the pub.

After a while, I gave up carrying the valise, simply dropped it on the side of the road and jammed my hands deep into my pockets. I'd turned up my coat collar to protect my neck and face as much as possible, but the icy breeze found every tiny bit of exposed skin. A gust tore the hat off my head and set it whirling across the moor, leaving my ears to burn with cold.

I hadn't been this miserable even on the night Richard came thundering up on his charger to rescue me, and there didn't seem to be much hope for a repeat performance of that. I was on my own under a sky full of billowing black clouds that turned the new day back into evening.

With every step, I thought of Madame Alijeva's words about how much power a dark spirit—demon, ghost, or what have you—could wield. I recalled more clearly the sense of gloom that had invaded me often when I'd first arrived and the time I'd awoken unable to move or breathe. After getting caught up in my affair with Richard, all that negativity had been too easy to forget. While I was having my fun, had Clive been attacked in the same ways? Had he suffered these moods in silence, thinking no one could help him?

I was a selfish man. Deep in my gut, I knew that while I'd been picking flowers with Richard, a storm had been gathering all around us. Something was about to happen and soon, maybe this very day.

Hurry. Hurry. You may already be too late.

Where had Lavinia and her pestering been these past weeks while I'd dallied with her husband? Madame had suggested the lady's spirit might be a captive of the much stronger evil entity. Perhaps she'd been unable to communicate with me, or perhaps I simply hadn't been listening anymore.

Thunder rumbled and lightning crackled through the gray billowing clouds, far too close for comfort. My legs were leaden, my body chilled so my teeth chattered, but I managed to pick up the pace and nearly jogged as I reached the drive leading to the Hall. Another nearby crash and flash made me flat-out run the final yards to the shelter of the building.

I went around to the servants' entrance since the front would be locked, and could barely shut the door behind me, the wind pushed so hard to keep it open. I rested for a moment, simply breathing and rubbing feeling back into my hands. Then I hurried into the kitchen to see if there was anything hot on the stove to eat or drink. A cup of tea to restore me, and I'd take up my duty again.

The kitchen was empty. Not even the scent of breakfast lingered. It was the first time I'd seen the room without Cook or the scullery maid in it. I grabbed an apple from the larder and crunched it down as I trotted upstairs.

The twins weren't in the schoolroom or their bedroom, and the notes I'd left for them were gone. So at least two people in the house knew I'd run away. I wondered if the boys were upset or sad. Maybe they were glad to finally be rid of me, although it *had* been some time since either had played a trick designed to drive me away.

The door to my room stood partially open. I entered and halted when I beheld Richard sitting on the edge of the bed, staring at the trunk I'd left behind.

He leaped up to confront me. "Where have you been? Smithers told me you'd left with your valise in hand. You would go with no word or letter of explanation, nothing?"

His fierce scowl would take the starch out of the bravest soul, but it no longer had the power to affect me. I knew his bark was worse than his bite. I knew many things about Richard Allinson.

I calmly took off the coat I still wore and hung it on a hook. "I came back," I answered simply. "I thought I owed it to the boys to see them off to school."

"Their mother left them suddenly and without explanation. It was cruel and thoughtless of you to even consider doing the same!"

"Oh, I left *them* a note." I stressed the pronoun.

His lips compressed, and he crossed his arms over his broad chest. "Yet not your employer, after I overlooked your lies?"

I raised an eyebrow. "Merely an employer, then? The rest of it meant nothing, an experience to be put behind you and forgotten?"

"I didn't say that. I…" He faltered. "It did mean something. I've grown very fond of you."

Don't humor me, I wanted to yell. But it was my own fault I'd allowed myself to grow attached when I always knew there was an end in sight for us.

Richard dropped his arms to his sides, his anger blown out like a strong wind. "I never wanted you to actually *leave*. I imagined somehow we'd find a way to continue to keep company. I offered you severance pay and a reference, but I didn't really mean to send you away. I simply hadn't yet figured out how we might carry on. But I pictured it."

I was pathetically pleased he'd entertained fantasies in which we continued to be together. He'd given that much thought to it. And I was disgusted with myself for caring.

"I almost followed you to tell you that. I should have. But you were so very angry, and my temper was up too. I thought it best to let our emotions cool and talk to you in the morning. When I came to your room and found your things gone..." He shook his head. "My heart was torn out at the thought of actually losing you. I realized how greatly I'd wronged you, particularly in the casual way I broke the news, and I apologize."

I nearly crumbled at the sorrowful look in his eyes, which had much more power over me than anger and yelling. But I wasn't quite ready to accept his belated apology.

I replied blandly, injecting all the nonchalance I could muster into my tone. "I reconsidered my rash action and returned. I'll prepare the boys for school and accept whatever recommendation you choose to give me when my work here is finished. Right now, I need to find Whit and Clive. They've hidden themselves away somewhere."

"Do they do that often?"

"Not so much as when I first got here, although recently Clive has reverted to disappearing for stretches of time." It was embarrassing to admit how little control I'd exerted over my charges. "There are many rooms in which to play hide-and-seek, and then, of course, there's their refuge in the garden."

Richard glanced at my windowpanes, which rattled in the strong, wet wind. "Not on a day like this."

I wasn't so sure. "If they're angry about me leaving, they might very well choose to run away to their special place. It's quite sheltered there." A sense of urgency gnawed at me. The boys had disappeared many times since I'd been here, but today felt different, as if they might be in some danger. Maybe it was simply Madame's letter unnerving me and the boys would pop back up on their own time as they always did. "At any rate, I should like to check the walled garden before searching the entire house."

"I'll go with you. I'll get my coat," Richard said as I headed for my own coat, which dripped water in a puddle on the floor.

He stopped before me and grasped my shoulders, forcing me to meet his gaze. "I am sorry I hurt you. I was on the verge of riding after you, catching you before you could leave the village. And I only raged upon seeing you because I was so relieved you weren't already on a train bound for someplace I might never find you. Please forgive me. Somehow we'll find a way to continue our friendship once you're no longer the boys' tutor. I swear I won't let you go so easily ever again."

Hope burned bright inside me, fluttering in my chest as it had in Pandora's box, eager to take flight. I swallowed my growing exultation at his declaration and managed a shrug. "I suppose I *might* forgive you. But I shall demand reparation for my mental pain and suffering. I can think of all sorts of *punishments* for a cad who would treat me so."

I batted my eyelashes coquettishly and earned a rumbling chuckle from Richard. "You may punish me in any way you see fit," he responded. "And I promise to utterly submit—and enjoy it."

His quick parting kiss turned into a longer one before finally we separated. I pushed at his hard chest and gasped. "We should hurry. Time for all that later."

Richard nodded. "I'll meet you at the rear entry."

After he left, I stood for a second grinning at the double entendre of *rear entry* and gripping my clammy wool coat. Maybe my running off in a huff had been for the best if it made Richard recognize his deeper feelings for me.

I shook off such giddy joy and put on my coat. Time to plunge into the foul weather again and search for my difficult, exasperating boys.

By the time we got outside and past the main garden, the rain had settled into a relentless downpour. Foolish to even imagine the twins would brave this storm, but they may have headed to the garden before it got this bad and decided to remain in that rocky grotto until the rain abated.

The wind lashed, and the sky was so overcast, it might have been night rather than day. A lantern to light our way would've been helpful, but we hadn't brought one, so we trudged through the murky gloom. Richard held aside the swag of vines that hid the garden's entrance, and I passed through the gap.

Once inside, the tall yew hedges cut the wind considerably. I wiped rain from my eyes and looked across the garden. The white angel statue seemed to glow faintly, guiding us to the grotto. The moss and dirt that normally shrouded her form seemed to be wiped away, and the marble shone as if brand-new. I told myself this transformation was from the heavy rain washing her clean, but in my heart, I knew it was more than that.

For the first time in days, I felt Lavinia's presence. Perhaps she'd depleted all her energy in her initial contacts with me and temporarily lost her ability to reach me. Or maybe here in her garden, she was beyond the control of the evil entity that would keep her silenced.

Whatever the explanation, I felt her beseeching message loud and clear in the midst of the pouring rain and growling thunder. *Find them! Protect them.*

I reached the statue and rested my hand on its feet as the boys had done so many times. *Show me where and tell me how.*

You know where.

Of course, I did. I'd known before coming here where this would ultimately end. Perhaps I'd merely hoped to avoid the confrontation a little longer. Thinking of facing evil in the abstract was one thing. Admitting it was a real force and trying to combat it was quite another. I wasn't at all ready to be so brave.

I turned to Richard. "I know where to find the boys. They're in the tower. And there's something I need to tell you. You're not going to want to believe it."

He touched the angel's wing tip and regarded its pale carved face. "I trust you to tell me the truth."

"Do you believe in spirits haunting the living?"

Richard wiped locks of wet black hair off his forehead and stared at me.

"It will sound outrageous, but this is what has happened to me since I've been here." I outlined the various odd occurrences, two of which Richard had witnessed for himself, the crashing candlestick in the chapel and the falling book. I told him of the messages Lavinia had given me, about the negative moods coming from beyond me and the times I'd awoken feeling I couldn't breathe. I shared the tale Tommy had told about the long-ago killer in the house. Then I gave him Madame Alijeva's explanation of the spirit world.

"I don't know if this thing is a demon or residual energy from a very evil man, but it *is* a real and threatening presence. It's dangerous and insidiously works its way into one's mind."

My impulse was to go on talking, trying to convince him by the sheer volume of my words, but I forced myself to fall silent and await his response. I cringed at his expression of doubt, which I could easily see despite the lack of light.

"You believe this…entity is what drove Lavinia to take her own life?" he finally asked.

"Maybe. Probably. I experienced firsthand that crushing feeling of hopelessness. It wasn't my own, I swear. It emanated from the thing in the tower. I only wish I'd tried harder to prevent its influence on Clive, although I'm not sure how. I think all we can do is get the boys out of the house as soon as possible."

"We are in agreement on that much. If I hadn't been so mired in my own despair, I would've understood sooner the boys needed a change." Richard glanced at the rooftops visible against the gray sky. "The Hall has never been a happy home. Nothing thrives in this place."

He didn't say he believed my tale of haunting but nodded. "Let us go find my sons."

CHAPTER 22

Inside the house, we shed our wet coats and muddy shoes in the back entry and headed toward the tower. We hadn't gone far beyond the kitchen before encountering Tom carrying a polishing rag and a stack of silver to the large table in the servants' hall. He looked from me to Richard and back again, his vacant gray eyes growing suddenly sharp.

"It's time," he muttered.

"Time for what, Tommy?" Richard asked gently.

Tom's gaze returned to me. "You know what to do?"

"Not really. I thought a cross and some sage to burn?"

I didn't question the boy's ability to know exactly what was happening. A dark and deadly feeling simmered around us in a thick and potent stew. Thrumming, humming electricity crackled in the very air, like the lightning outdoors. Danger. Trouble. Fear.

Tom nodded. "I'll get some herbs." He dropped the armload of silver on the table with a clanging clatter and hurried into the kitchen.

"Catch up with us," I called after him and tugged on Richard's sleeve. "We need a religious icon or cross. I thought of the one on the chapel altar, though it's very heavy. Do you have anything else?"

"Do you honestly believe—" he began.

"I don't know what I believe. But we should be armed with

everything we can, just in case. Baptismal water would be good, but I suppose regular water might do for purification."

"These are your psychic friend's suggestions?" His mouth twisted in a skeptical smirk.

"Some of them, but she said the most important tool to combat evil is love." I winced at how clichéd that sounded.

My sense of urgency grew. We'd stood talking for too long. Time to *move*, to perform some sort of action. I stopped worrying about convincing Richard, and we headed toward the chapel.

As we passed near Richard's bedroom, he said, "Give me a moment."

He went inside and emerged soon after with a lamp, which he gave to me. He brandished an iron fireplace poker like a sword. "My nanny used to tell ghost tales. She said iron repels them, which is why churchyards have iron fences, to keep any spirits that would wander contained."

His gesture touched me. I could tell Richard didn't believe or only slightly believed me, yet he trusted me enough to go along with my mad story. I smiled my gratitude before hurrying on.

With every step farther into the medieval part of the building, my anxiety and unease grew. It was as if we drew closer to the source of all negative energy. The air grew freezing and the corridor darker, devouring the small light cast from the lamp. The hair on my neck rose like a dog's hackles, and the primitive desire to run from danger vibrated through me. I glanced at Richard to see if he too experienced a feeling of impending danger. If he was sensitive to it, I couldn't read it on his impassive face.

We entered the chapel. The simple stone cross was no more than two feet tall, but the granite was so heavy, I could barely lift it from the altar.

Richard handed me the poker and hefted the cross in both arms.

He cradled it against his chest and glanced at me. "You're certain we need this?"

"It couldn't hurt." I picked up the lamp in my free hand and clutched the poker tightly in the other.

The moment we left the quiet sanctuary and approached the tower again, my feeling of panic resumed. I recalled the swirling dark mist that had manifested when I was in the tower, the stench of rotten meat and the feeling of pure evil that had oozed from it. After that experience, I'd let myself forget, but now those memories rolled over me in waves. What could we do against a formless thing, an entity that seemed old and strong and too terrible to be a mere ghost? I was powerless and incapable of doing anything useful to save the boys.

On the heels of that thought, I understood this was the entity polluting my mind again, filling me with self-doubt and hopelessness. I must cast off such debilitating feelings and be strong—for Clive and Whitney, and for Richard too.

I looked over at him. He smiled at me, and I drew strength from the warm feeling that filled me. *Love conquers evil.* Madame had written something like that. I could only pray it was true and not a wishful platitude.

We rounded a corner to face the door to the tower, closed as I'd left it. Recalling that bleak darkness that had assailed me last time, the very last thing I wanted to do was confront it again.

"It's unusually cold," Richard murmured, the mist of his breath floating on the air.

I clenched my chattering teeth and held the lamp higher, but it barely cast a light in the gloom.

Richard set the heavy cross on the floor and turned the latch. The door wouldn't budge. He tried again, pulling harder. Still it wouldn't open.

"It's not locked. The same thing happened to me in the tower before, as if someone held the door closed."

Richard studied the door, then held out his hand. "Give me the poker."

I handed it over, and he drove the tip up under the top hinge in the groove where the door met the wall. He began to pry. A few tugs and grunts, and he'd popped the nails from the door. The hinge flopped open. He did the same to the lower one, wedging in the poker and prying it loose.

But two broken hinges made the door no easier to open. Richard began to whack at the handle, then tried to pry the iron tip into the jamb. He cursed as the door defied all his attempts to get it open, and the sense of impending danger made every wasted second feel like an hour.

Footsteps approached down the corridor. Tom arrived, bearing a bundle of dried herbs and a glass container of water. He'd come armed with matches and struck one to set fire to the bundle. Smoke rose from the flaming herbs. Tom waved the herbal smudge in front of the door. The scent of burning sage and lavender surrounded Richard and me, the smoke stinging our eyes.

If there was some blessing, prayer, or incantation we were supposed to chant, Madame hadn't shared it. So I extemporized, calling out, "By the power of God and all his saints, by the power of love and, um, humanity, I command you to open this door. I deny your power and refute your authority. Let go, you bloody wanker!"

Richard leaned all his weight into the iron poker wedged between the door and its frame, and suddenly, the heavy wooden door popped loose. Both Tom and I jumped back to avoid it. Richard took a glancing blow to the shoulder and cried out with pain. The door crashed to the floor, and the black maw of the stairwell stood like an open mouth waiting to swallow us whole.

Clammy coldness rolled out from that darkness, making our breath steam. And the cold was suffused with a sense of menace beyond any rational explanation.

Richard rubbed his shoulder and gazed into the stairwell. "How can the boys be up there? We could scarcely open the door." But he sounded as if he were trying to convince himself.

"You feel it, don't you?" I asked. "That evil thing holds sway here. It allows in who it wants and bars the way to others." I put a hand on his sore shoulder. "Will you be all right?"

Richard grunted and handed off the poker to me. He bent to pick up the heavy cross once more. "Tom, you needn't come with us. Stay down here where it's…safe." He spoke the last word reluctantly, as if he still couldn't believe he was buying into this ghost story.

Tom dropped the remains of the smoking bundle of herbs to the floor before they burned his fingertips. He held up his jar of water. "For cleansing evil spirits, Gran said. I'll do it."

"Very well." Richard shifted the cross to lean against his good shoulder and also took the lantern before walking into the stairwell. I followed right behind him.

It was like entering a butcher's ice house. The stench of carcasses surrounded us. The air felt thick as water. Each step forward was an effort as we slowly ascended the stairs, and the lantern's light was swallowed in darkness. I could hardly see Richard right in front of me, or Tom when I glanced behind.

Time seemed fluid and strange the way it is when one is feverish. In what felt like days but was probably only minutes, we reached the landing at the top of the stairs and faced the second door. This one stood wide open like a challenge, as if the creature that dwelled there was toying with us. *You want to enter here? Come along in, then.*

My throat was so tight, I could hardly swallow, and my chest ached from the pounding of my heart. I suddenly knew exactly what we would find—two little boys hanging from a rafter beam. A whimper escaped me at the thought.

But no. Even with the chair, they couldn't manage to sling a rope over the beam to hang themselves. The idea they might have followed the same course as their mother was impossible.

Richard stopped in front of me so abruptly, I ran into his broad back. I peered around him.

The room with its single chair was not empty this time. Whitney stood perched on the wide sill of one of the tall windows with Clive beside him on the floor. Rain pounded on the roof and streamed past the other windows, yet none entered the room. This space seemed isolated from the world outside, wrapped in cotton that deafened my hearing and fogged my vision. Although it was only a few yards across the room to where the boys were, they were indistinct shapes. A great black formless mass filled the room. We were flies buzzing straight into its web.

"Whitney, come away from the window," Richard called. "Clive, come to me, son."

Whitney seemed not to hear and remained silhouetted in the window, but Clive slowly turned to face us. His body pivoted in an unnatural way, and his eyes seemed to glow in his small, pale face. His mouth opened, and a man's voice came from him. "Call me not your son, you vile perversion."

I gasped at the shocking sound of that deep, adult voice emerging from a child's mouth.

"Performing your filthy acts, rubbing and grasping at each other. Copulating like animals," the voice sneered, and Clive's features twisted in pure disgust. "And they considered *me* evil. I, who merely collected women."

A hiccup of laughter escaped me. I couldn't help it. My default reaction when terrorized to the point of wetting my drawers was to laugh.

The thing inside Clive turned its blazing eyes on me, and every bone in my body went liquid. I thought I'd collapse.

"You would laugh at *me*?" It growled—literally growled—with a reverberating sound that filled the room.

I shook my head. "No. You're very formidable. I was merely thinking your copulations ended in the demise of your partners. I imagine the ladies hardly found it satisfying."

The thing in Clive's body took a step toward me, its anger rolling over me in hot waves. "I *never* had relations with either female or *male*. I wouldn't defile my body that way."

"Of course." I swallowed hard and checked on Tom, who stood to my left, clutching his jar of would-be holy water and gaping. On my other side, Richard set down the lantern as he stared at the Clive-thing. At the moment, neither of my allies was in any condition to help.

"So, you've taken a new body," I said. "Starting over again?"

Could the evil thing hold Clive hostage indefinitely? Could it continue to inhabit Clive while keeping Whit in some sort of trance? Madame had given me no possession lore beyond the bit I'd learned about psychic channeling, but it seemed to me this would require a great draw of energy that would need to be replenished.

The creature perambulated Clive closer to us—awkwardly, as if controlling flesh after so many years of incorporeal form was difficult. The boy's jerky marionette steps were so horrifying to witness, I no longer felt remotely like laughing.

Richard recovered at last, lifted the stone cross with both hands, and thrust it toward Clive. "Begone, creature! Release my son."

The thing emitted a creaky sound meant to be laughter. It grinned, stretching Clive's mouth too wide. "My power is beyond your imagining. You cannot expel me. I possess this body and will dispose of the other." He lifted an arm and pointed at Whit, who swayed in the window, no longer bracing his hands against the frame.

"No!" Richard yelled. He dropped the cross onto the flagstones with a crash that sent bits of granite flying and lunged toward Whitney. But the very air held Richard back, and he moved in slow motion, as if mired in sticky mud.

In the face of this powerful evil thing that seemed to be much more than the mere ghost of a killer, I felt like an infant. We'd come armed with a poker, a cross, and a vial of not-holy water. We were ridiculous.

"You are nothing," the creature spat. "A pervert too weak to fight his sick desires, an imbecile fit only to scrub away shit, and a liar worth nothing at all."

A thick rush of horrible feelings crowded me, useless, inadequate, powerless, unworthy. I'd fought to overcome these adjectives all my life. Damned if I'd let them emasculate me now. I recalled something else Madame Alijeva had told me before. *Evil will find weakness and strike there.* She'd said hidden flaws and secrets would be used against a person, a little truth intermingling with lies to make the victim doubt himself.

I still fought a daily battle against the sense of worthlessness instilled in me by Roger Dwyer, but I would not allow this creature to exploit it today.

"I *believe* I deserve love," I declared loudly. "And I've found it with Richard and Whitney and Clive. I love all of them."

Did I see the Clive-thing wince at the mention of love? I tested my theory.

"I *love* them, and they *love* me. We're like a family." I dropped the poker and threw an arm around Tom, who still stood beside me, clutching the jar of water. "I love Tom too. We're all simply full of *love*, something an evil being can never fathom or vanquish."

"Craven feelings! You lust after these boys' young bodies. You'd love to touch them in foul ways, wouldn't you?" it sneered.

"At the moment, I'd like to punch Clive in the mouth, but only because you're inhabiting him."

I darted a glance at Richard, who continued to move toward Whitney like a fly stuck in jelly. He needed time, and I needed to distract the Clive-thing. I removed my arm from around Tom's shoulders but not before giving him a squeeze to get him moving.

Tom finally stopped staring at Clive to look at me, and I flicked my eyes toward the water jar.

"Why now?" I asked. "You've haunted this tower—this entire house—for decades. Why choose now to manifest?"

Evil things apparently love to talk about themselves. Something Madame had neglected to mention. The spirit didn't hesitate to expound.

"The perfect opportunity arose, first with the woman, so weak and easy to manipulate, as are all of her sex. Convincing her to kill herself was a pleasure. And this boy, as miserable as both his parents, so *easy* to make my pawn."

Richard was only a few feet away from Whit now and still strained toward him. His body pressed as if making headway in a strong wind.

"You tried it with me, didn't you?" I continued to involve the thing in conversation while Tom unscrewed the lid of the jar and dipped out water. "But you gave up when I wouldn't crumble and went after Clive instead."

"The purity of this vessel was preferable to the defiled body you inhabit." Clive flung up a hand, and the jar of water flew out of Tom's hands. It shot up toward the ceiling, cracked against the same beam Lavinia had likely hanged herself on, and crashed to the ground. Shards scattered like bullets.

Tom dropped to his knees amidst the broken glass and tried to scoop water from the puddle on the floor. He mumbled a prayer and flicked droplets of water mingled with blood from his cut fingertips toward Clive. He prayed louder. "Holy Father, protect us from evil, free us from darkness, cover us with your great light."

It seemed Tom's pitiful ritual couldn't possibly do any good against something so powerful. And yet, Clive hissed when one drop of bloodied water hit his cheek. He stepped back and gave another animalistic growl.

Faith. You must have it even if you do not believe. Madame's conundrum wafted through my mind.

"Well, I'll be damned," I murmured.

I didn't know any formal prayers, but I could back Tom with a show of support. "Holy Spirit, be with us. Come upon us like a…like a dove and bring your…heavenly light."

I bent and hauled the altar cross up in my arms, nearly wrenching my back from its weight. I cradled the stone to my chest like a child and tried to believe it stood for something.

It did, I realized. To generations of people convinced some prophet died to save their souls in an act of ultimate selflessness. Whether it actually happened or not didn't matter. And the vicious battles over doctrine waged over hundreds of years didn't matter. All that mattered was the kernel of truth—sacrifice of one man for the greater good.

I could do that. I *would* do that for Richard and Clive and Whit, if it meant they escaped this place unharmed.

"Take me," I blurted. "Let Clive go. I'll become your vessel without resistance. Wouldn't an adult man be better for achieving your goals? With Clive, you'd have to wait years before you could begin your, um, collection again. His body is small and incapable of controlling your quarry."

I hardly planned my words. I only hoped I might lure the thing to abandon Clive. Tom and Richard could get the boys out of the house. What might happen to me afterward didn't bear thinking about. I'd never been brave or heroic, but I was ready to give it a go that day.

Miraculously, the thing appeared to be considering my proposition. "Put the cross down."

I leaned to set the cross on its base on the floor, then made the mistake of glancing at Richard. He had hold of Whit's wrist and was about to tug him inside the room. Clive followed my look. With a howl of rage, he flung up his hand once more.

Whit plummeted from the window as if he'd been shoved. Richard clung to him, using all his strength to fight gravity and haul Whit back over the sill.

At the same instant, Tom rushed toward Clive. He produced a container of salt from his jacket pocket, which he poured in a misshapen white circle around the boy. The creature howled and tossed Tom through the air with a flick of its power. Tom's back smashed against the wall, and he fell to the floor in a heap—but not before the circle was complete.

The Clive-thing tried to move forward but seemed to be contained as if by an iron fence. It continued to scream in impotent rage, shouting curses and threats in English and in a foreign tongue that sounded as ancient as the world.

Richard had Whitney in his arms, cradled against his chest. The boy clung to his father and wept, the creature's power over him broken. The very air seemed clearer; the stench of a charnel house dissipated. But Clive was still trapped with an evil spirit inside him. I could think of only one way to separate them.

"My offer stands. Release the boy and use me instead. If you promise to do that, I'll step inside the circle."

Red-faced and wild-eyed, Clive stopped ranting and focused on me, the thing inside him recovering its temper and assessing me coldly. "Very well."

Tom, who'd staggered to his feet, grabbed my arm. "Don't trust it."

"How else can we set Clive free?" I searched for some clever way I might outwit the enemy without sacrificing myself, but nothing came to me.

Then I smelled the scent of lavender.

"It will claim you both," Tom warned.

"Graham, don't do it!" Richard shouted as he put down Whitney and headed toward me.

I stepped over the thin stream of white, such a fragile barrier to hold a demon prisoner, I could hardly believe it worked. Immediately, I felt the thick negative energy surround me again. Evil, plain and simple. Madame Alijeva was right. Such things existed whether one wanted to believe in them or not.

But so did goodness. I braced myself to demonstrate my own brand of faith, forced myself to relax, and waited for energy to flow in.

What transpired next is hard to put into limited human words. When concepts like time, space, and reality are fluid and slippery, it's difficult to assign a linear order to things. The Evil—I could only think of it as that now—poured into me, my body, my spirit, and I knew all it had done, all it was capable of doing. I saw the acts it had performed when it lived in that long-ago Allinson, not only in this tower room but other places as well. I *felt* the thrill of the hunt, the capture, the torture, the possession, the kill.

He (I) spotted a woman, alone and defenseless, herding her cattle home for the evening. We stalked her and presented ourselves, knowing she'd not dare show rudeness to the young master of the estate. She seemed flattered by our attention, went with us willingly like one of her dumb cows, and then was surprised when we tied her up.

The look in her eyes, *stupid, ignorant, animal eyes*, as she saw the knife and understood she was about to suffer was exquisite. We wanted to treasure that moment forever, put it in a box, and take it out to savor again and again. After that, she existed only at our whim. We owned her and demonstrated it in many ways with the blade. Carved her, stabbed her, probed her in the secret places she could no longer keep hidden. All of her exposed to our omniscience. We prolonged this as long as possible, and at the final moment when the light would flicker out in her eyes, ours was the last face she saw—and we knew we possessed her completely.

The creature's satisfaction equaled that of climax and sickened the part that was still me, Joe Green, Graham Cowrie, human man. I screamed for help before Evil engulfed me completely and forever. And help arrived as I'd betted it would. I might not have thrown all my chips in the pot otherwise.

When I'd sensed Lavinia near me before I'd stepped into the circle, I'd begged her assistance in defeating the horrible entity threatening her child. Now I gave myself over to her, and her energy joined with mine.

Just as I'd felt in a flash the full experience of what it meant to be Evil—not only one murder but every kill and the entire history of the black entity—now I experienced what being Lavinia meant.

I felt her as a young girl with dreams of love and family, her hopes as she'd gone to her wedding bed, her disappointment in Richard, her deep love for the children she bore. All of her life and the bleak misery of her death exploded in one powerful burst of understanding. But in the morass of her feelings, Love—the sort with a capital L—was strongest. Hers and mine together could prove formidable.

My body became a battleground, but I wasn't helpless. The negative energy continued to invade me, bleakness and despair attempting to control me, but a pure light filled me to counteract it.

At the same time this inner struggle waged, I was dimly aware of Clive collapsing like an abandoned doll, Richard carrying him away, Tom taking Whitney out of the room. Richard returned after sending the others away and came to my aid, shouting my name and physically trying to reach me. I saw all these things take place, but they meant little compared to the more esoteric action taking place within me.

Love and Evil were at war, my spirit the stake in their battle. But Mr. Evil, after however many millennia it had existed, still seemed to misunderstand a simple fact. Souls weren't helpless booty to be fought over. I wasn't the sacrificial cow-maiden for it to possess. I, me, useful Joe Green, threw up a barrier and shoved back. I would not be owned or used, tortured or enslaved. I summoned the Love inside me like a secret weapon and wielded a blade of great power against Evil.

Poets and holy men have said love conquers all. It is stronger and greater than anything. When one believes in its power and pours his entire essence into that belief, all things are possible. Together, Lavinia's spirit and mine, overflowing with love for Clive, combined and beat back the darkness. We drove it, howling, out of my head. And then it just…winked out, evaporated like the final shadows of night disappearing under the full glow of a new day.

I collapsed on the floor, completely emptied, shaken, and as exhausted as if I'd run to London and back. My brain was my own again. I could think and feel with no other presence but mine inhabiting my head, not even Lavinia's. No inner voices, no darkness or light, no more of other people's memories crowding mine. Only me, and I was glad to have myself to myself once more. In fact, I quite loved Me just then.

"Graham! Graham, are you all right?" Richard shouted right in my face, and I realized he'd been trying to get me to hear him for some time.

"I would be if you'd quit yelling at me," I answered groggily.

I was crushed in his arms, squashed so hard against him I couldn't draw breath. He hugged me tightly and actually swept me off my feet to carry me from the room. I threw my arms around his neck and prayed he wouldn't try to carry me down those steep, curving stairs like some rescued maiden. We'd never make it without falling.

But he set me on my feet on the landing.

Tom had gone ahead with the children. We stood clinging to each other for a moment before Richard took my face between his hands and kissed me tenderly.

"You saved my sons," he murmured. "And you saved me, in so many ways. I didn't realize how lost I was until you brought me back into the world. Back to happiness. I love you and never want to be without you, Graham Cowrie, Joe Green, or whatever you want to call yourself."

As he kissed me again, the door to the tower room swung softly closed, and from the far side, I swore I heard the quiet echo of a woman's laughter.

CHAPTER 23

We never knew if the evil that lurked in Allinson Hall was permanently banished, but it seemed, at the very least, to be in hibernation. To ensure the tower room remained undisturbed, Richard barred the door with boards nailed across it. Perhaps more importantly, he, Tom, and I carried the angel statue from Lavinia's garden and stationed it in front of that boarded entrance. I polished the marble till it shone in the gloom.

The statue might have only been a symbol, but we *believed* it was a ward to keep any residual evil sealed up. And if I'd learned nothing else through the ordeal, it was that belief was a powerful thing.

We kept Whitney and Clive close to one or the other of us for the few days we remained in the house. Richard dismissed the remaining servants with bonus pay and good references and declared he'd stay at the Hall for only a few days at a time when he needed to come and check up on the estate. He sent Tom on ahead to the London house, promising him a home forever.

"You're part of our family, not just a servant." Richard clapped Tom on the shoulder after giving him instructions and a train ticket. "We couldn't manage without you. And I hope that you'll keep creating your beautiful artwork so that I might have it framed and hung throughout the house."

Tom's smile transformed his homely face to one as beautiful as the marble angel. He nodded vigorously and went to pack for his trip.

The next day, Richard and I watched the boys take a last run along the paths of the secluded garden. "I'd happily burn the house to the ground before we go," he admitted to me.

"I don't think stone would burn," I pointed out, "but yes, I'd like to tear it down to the foundations myself. I wonder if that creature would continue to haunt the ruins. Would we have to salt the earth to purify it?"

I also wondered about Lavinia. Did her spirit still linger even though she'd set her family to rights? I hadn't heard or felt her since that moment on the staircase. Her quiet laughter had seemed like a period on a sentence, and I felt fairly confident she'd moved on to someplace much nicer than a dismal tower.

Clive came barreling up the path and threw his arms around his father's waist. Flushed and breathless, he grinned up at him. "Your turn to be it."

"We weren't even playing," Richard protested. "Go catch your brother."

"Can't. He's too fast."

Richard ruffled his hair. "Very well. I'll count to ten to give you a head start, but don't run too far from me."

Clive hared off, a normal, healthy, happy nine-year-old boy. Happier now the boys knew they wouldn't be going to boarding school for a while yet. Richard couldn't bear to ship them off, and I'd convinced him an extra year or even two with private tutoring at home wouldn't ruin them.

I'd said to him, "I understand how it is with the gentry. You solidify your place in society with the connections you make as early as your primary school days. But let them be carefree children for a bit longer. I wish I'd had that opportunity, don't you?"

Richard capitulated easily and scheduled a trip to the seaside before our return to London.

Now Richard finished his counting and ran after Clive and Whit, who scattered to opposite ends of the garden. They darted like sparrows evading a hawk. Their sharp maneuvers kept them just out of reach, since barging across the garden beds was forbidden in the game.

Richard chased them for a while, then began to run toward me. I yelped and stopped standing and gawping like a fool. I raced pell-mell up one path and down another with Richard always on my heels.

I rounded a corner and ran full tilt into Whitney coming the other way. We crashed together and fell to the ground in a tangle of legs. Richard showed no mercy but tagged us both.

"We can't both be it," I huffed and drew a breath into my aching lungs. I had a stitch in my side, and a bruise would be forming on my elbow where I'd slammed it into the stone, but I couldn't have been happier.

Richard reached out a hand to both of us and pulled us to our feet.

"Can we swim when we get to the seashore?" Whit asked. "Will there be shells?" He'd been asking the same questions ever since he learned about the holiday we were about to embark on.

"It's too cold. You know that," Clive said as he came to join us. "We won't be able to go in at all. But maybe we can take a boat ride?" He looked hopefully at his father.

"I'm certain we may." Richard smiled at Clive, at both of the boys, and then gave me a wink. "We'll find plenty of ways to enjoy our time by the sea."

"After that, we go home to our London house," Whit confirmed.

"That's right. We'll spend a lot of time together going to parks and museums and the botanical gardens."

"We'll see the Egyptian mummies," Whit declared at the same time Clive said, "The Royal Academy. I want to see the paintings."

"All the museums," Richard assured them. "And if you'd like to take classes in some special interest such as painting or archeology, we can arrange that."

Clive caught hold of my hand. "Mr. Cowrie can teach us. We don't want him to go away."

Richard exchanged a look with me over their heads. "No. We wouldn't want to lose a valuable man like Mr. Cowrie. He'll continue to teach the basic subjects. When you finally go to school, I believe he'll stay on as my personal secretary. I can always use help with…correspondence and such."

"I do write a beautiful hand," I said with a smile.

"We should leave today instead of tomorrow," Clive said. "I don't want to wait."

I wondered if the boy had any recollection of what had happened, his possession. We'd given him every opportunity to talk about it—no more secrets or keeping mum—but neither he nor Whit seemed to remember. Either the twins had blocked those memories, or they'd been mentally elsewhere during that horrible ordeal in the tower room. At any rate, it seemed all of us had had enough of dwelling in the past and only wanted to focus on a much brighter future.

Richard considered the tasks he still needed to accomplish on the estate before he left, but nodded. "It's a little late in the day to start out, but we should be able to take the last train to Scarborough and travel the next day to Whitby and our rental by the sea."

"We never have to come here again?" Whitney asked.

"Never again," his father promised.

The seashore in a North Country winter is hardly inviting. Slate-gray water capped with white froth crashes against the stony strand, and the wind cuts like a blade. Definitely too cold to wade in that thick, icy water, but the boys enjoyed roaming the shore, picking up broken shells and ocean-smoothed stones. Richard and I enjoyed watching them explore as we strolled a short distance behind.

There were no holiday crowds, very few people at all that time of year. Sometimes we'd watch fishermen coming in with full nets or unloading their catch on the wharf. Sometimes we'd be forced to seek shelter indoors, and we'd eat hot meat pies or seafood dishes at the local tavern. Other times we'd stay at our rental house and play card games in the parlor or read aloud a Robin Hood tale.

When the boys were occupied with their own books or games, Richard and I might take a moment to "search for something we needed" in his room or mine. Richard did quite a lot of groveling to show how sorry he was for nearly letting me go, though we had no opportunity to do *all* the things we would've liked. A few snatched moments of kissing and touching merely stoked desire, like feeding tiny bits of coal to a blazing fire. Even at night we didn't feel comfortable sneaking into each other's beds—not in this small house with the twins so nearby.

But I comforted myself with the knowledge that once we were ensconced in the Kensington house, we'd create an arrangement that suited our needs while keeping our behavior beyond reproach for the sake of the staff.

"We should rent a flat," Richard mentioned one day in his room after he'd kissed warmth back into my chapped lips. "A place we can go where no one will ask questions and we can do as we please."

"Mm," I murmured, too sated with kissing to give a proper reply. But part of me recalled the last time I'd been set up in an apartment and how awful I'd felt when that relationship ended.

I stroked my palm along Richard's rough cheek and rested it on his throat, feeling his heartbeats in my hand. "That would be nice, though I should rather feel like a kept man."

"And you would be. I would keep you *always*. Sharing a bedroom in my house if I could, claiming you as mine in front of the world. But since that's not possible, this is the only alternative I can come up with." He smoothed my shirt, which had gotten quite rumpled from our grappling embrace. "You would live in our house, acting the part of tutor or personal secretary, but we would be able to use the apartment whenever we chose."

"That would be nice," I repeated.

He searched my eyes with his dark gaze. "Are you afraid I would behave like that Leighton, who so foolishly tossed you away? That will *never* happen, I swear. My feelings for you will only grow deeper with time. I will be loyal to you in the way I would have devoted myself to Lavinia—if only I could have loved her the way she deserved to be loved. Loyalty is one good quality I'll admit to possessing."

I smiled. I shouldn't have needed to hear his promise, but I did. It was hard for me to trust those I loved would remain as enamored of me. I'd lost my father—although admittedly through no fault of his own—and then my mother when she'd chosen her lover over her own children. Leighton's abandonment had been the last straw, and I hadn't put out my trusting heart to be trampled again.

Until Richard.

"I believe you," I said at last. "I should be honored to share your house *and* your flat for the rest of our natural lives."

And beyond, if such was the way of the supernatural world.

ABOUT BONNIE DEE

Whether you're a fan of contemporary, historical, fantasy, gay or straight romance, you'll find something to enjoy among my books. I'm interested in flawed, often damaged, people who find the fulfillment they seek in one another. To learn more about my extensive backlist go to http://bonniedee.com. Find me on Facebook and Twitter @Bonnie_Dee.

Titles by Bonnie Dee
Phin's Christmas
The Artist
The Medium
The Fortune Hunter
The Masterpiece
The Tutor
The Copper
The Au Pair Affair
Jungle Heat
Peter and Wendell
Undeniable Magnetism
Cage Match
Caring for Riggs
Chilling with Max
Snow Angels with Bear
The Cowboy and the City Slicker

Titles by Bonnie Dee & Summer Devon
Seducing Stephen
The Gentleman and the Rogue
The Nobleman and the Spy
Sin and the Preacher's Son
The Psychic and the Sleuth
The Gentleman's Keeper
The Gentleman's Madness
Mending Him
The Bohemian and the Banker
Simon and the Christmas Spirit
Will and the Valentine Saint
Mike and the Spring Awakening
Delaney and the Autumn Masque

If you enjoyed The Tutor, check out this excerpt from The Masterpiece.

Built from the bottom up: one perfect gentleman.

Man about town Arthur Lawton spends his days pursuing entertainment while shoeshine Joe Sprat labors to better his family's lives. When an argument about nature versus nurture sparks a wager, Arthur swears to a friend he can turn this working man into a gentleman who will pass at a society function.

Joe is happy to participate in the experiment for a fee but receives more than he bargained for after moving into Lawton's house. Arthur is determined Joe won't merely wear a veneer of sophistication but educates him in every way. As he creates his new and improved man, Arthur grows more deeply infatuated with him, while Joe falls equally hard for his charismatic mentor.

Underneath a growing friendship, desire simmers and one day explodes. After their relationship escalates, the pair exists in a dream bubble until the threat of exposure sharply reminds them they belong in different worlds. When the ball is over, each must resume his own life, changed by their encounter but destined for different courses.

Find out if love is strong enough to bridge the gap between peer and pauper in this twist on the tale of My Fair Lady.

*

The butler pointed out a chair for him to sit in—not one of the upholstered armchairs but a wooden one with no fabric for him to dirty. He told Joe the master would be in presently then left the room.

Joe sat still for all of a minute but he wanted to see that fancy radiator up close. He pulled aside the screen and studied it then put the screen back and wandered around the room admiring other marvels. There was a fully-rigged sailing ship in a glass bottle on the mantle. Above that, a large portrait of a uniformed man with enormous mutton chop whiskers glared down at the intruder in the house.

"My grandfather, Admiral Cornelius Bingley Lawton. When I was a boy, he would bring me treasures from his trips to all corners of the globe."

The voice from behind Joe nearly made him jump out of his shoes. He turned to face Mr. Lawton, who had the same striking features and piercing eyes as the man in the painting.

"Please, sit down," Lawton indicated one of two armchairs facing the fireplace.

"Sorry, sir. I should've stayed where I was put, but this room…Cor, I ain't seen nothin' like it in me life. 'Tis a marvel." He went where Lawton directed and perched on the edge of the chair.

Lawton leaned back in his seat and gracefully crossed his long legs. "You may as well begin to learn proper etiquette. It's all right to be curious, but one doesn't generally poke about someone's house when paying a call."

The reprimand was not harshly spoken but it embarrassed Joe to be considered so ignorant. "I know, sir. It ain't considered polite among my sort either. I won't do it again."

Lawton studied him with those shining brown eyes. "You understand the terms of my wager with Lord Granville? In six weeks you will attend Lady Granville's spring gala as my guest. The social elite will be there, peers and politicians, perhaps even royalty. You must be as polished and well-spoken as any man there. If you convince them you're one of them, the proof will be in invitations to other social gatherings."

"Yes, sir. I understand." But he didn't really. It was an odd measure for winning a bet, especially when that Lord Muckety Granville seemed to be in charge of deciding whether Joe had passed muster or not.

Lawton continued in that smooth voice that stroked like velvet against Joe's ears, making the hair on his neck and arms pleasantly prickle. "As we proceed with your education, if I should correct you on any matter, it is without malice or intent to demean you. I don't know how much you know about the social graces I'll be attempting to impart."

"Yes, sir," Joe repeated, as it seemed the safest answer to give to all those high flown, fancy words. He didn't want to ruin this opportunity to earn twenty quid within his first minutes here. Lawton might choose some other bloke to train up and Joe would be booted out of the miracle he'd lucked into.

"This is about much more than a different way of speaking. There are rules governing even the most mundane behaviors in society, all of which must become second nature to you."

Lawton leaned forward now, his arms resting on his thighs and his gaze even more powerful. Joe felt it pressing against his chest like a hand. "But beyond that, there is a certain way you must carry yourself, with poise, confidence and dignity. I know quite a few pedigreed men, especially young bucks, who lack that air of quality. I want you to outmatch those of the highest breeding, to show what you are capable of through sheer willpower. Can you do that?"

Joe began nodding even before Lawton finished speaking. He hadn't felt the force of someone's words this way since his mum used to drag him to church where the minister's sermons on hellfire seemed directed at him. While that had scared the bejeezus out of him, Mr. Lawton's words lit him on fire. *I will become that man, the one with poise and confidence.*

"Yes! I'll do my very best for you, Mr. Lawton."

Lawton slapped Joe's knee. "Good man." He leaned back, but Joe still felt that warm touch.

"We'll start from the skin outward." The gentleman lightened his tone. "A bath and a fresh set of clothing. My tailor will come tomorrow to take your measurements for new clothing. For this evening, you may wear some of my clothes."

Joe noted his host's linen shirt, soft woolen trousers, jacket, and silk waistcoat, and had the silly thought of joining Lawton inside those clothes. He ducked his face to hide his smile at the absurd thought.

Lawton rose and went to the wall to press a button. "This is how you must summon a servant should you need one. A bell rings in the kitchen, letting the staff know in which room service is required. I'm fairly certainly Merton is hovering out in the hall just now, waiting to show you to the guest bedroom, and then to the washroom where a bath will be drawn." He frowned. "You *are* familiar with indoor plumbing? You've had a full bath before, not just washed up in a basin?"

What sort of conditions did he think Joe lived in? "Yes, sir. I've had tub baths. Not so large as yours, I imagine." *In a shared washroom for everyone on that floor and with lukewarm water only a few inches deep.* "I believe I can manage."

Lawton smiled and acknowledged his tone. "Sarcasm is a gentleman's rapier with which he fences daily. Point to you."

Merton came to collect Joe, and Joe lost track of time as one new experience after another rushed at him. He barely had time to take in the beautiful bed and lovely furnishings in the guest room before he was shown to the wash room.

There, he stood thunderstruck, staring from a huge claw-foot tub on a raised platform, with spigots for both cold and *hot* water, to the plush towels hung on a rack for the bather's convenience, to a large sink with an oval mirror in a curved frame above it.

His reflection gaped back at him, as grubby as a ragpicker or a homeless beggar. No wonder Lawton took him for an ignorant bum rather than a workingman who made a more or less adequate living.

"Do you require aide with your bath, Mr. Sprat," Merton interrupted his thoughts. "I could send Mr. Lawton's valet, Jackson, or one of the footmen."

"I can wash meself, thanks much." Joe cleared his throat and mimicked Lawton's plummy drawl, "You may leave now, my good man."

With the door closed behind Merton, Joe stripped off his clothes and tested the steaming water. He'd never in his life had so much water to splash around in except for an occasional swim in the filthy Thames on a hot summer day. He put in a toe, then a foot, then submerged his whole body right up to the chin in that glorious warmth. With a sigh, Joe closed his eyes and fell back, dousing his head. For a few moments, he floated underwater, allowing the heat to seep into his very bones and the water to soak the grime of the streets off him. Heavenly bliss!

At last he reached for the flannel and the fragrant bar of soap and began to scrub. He would step out of this bath a new man, ready to take on the world—or at least the better half of it. He would make Mr. Lawton proud with how easily he learned grammar and good manners. And he would make his mum even prouder when he opened a shop of his own at last.

Printed in Great Britain
by Amazon